THE HAUNTING

Best wishes.

T. Morley.

2016

THE HAUNTING

by

Thomas Morley

authorHOUSE®

AuthorHouse™
1663 Liberty Drive
Bloomington, IN 47403
www.authorhouse.com
Phone: 1-800-839-8640

Published by AuthorHouse   02/13/2013

ISBN: 978-1-4678-9656-6 (sc)
ISBN: 978-1-4678-9655-9 (hc)
ISBN: 978-1-4678-9657-3 (e)

For our Cal

I wish to thank the people who are an inspiration to my research: Kenneth Burnley for *Sanctuary in The Sea*; Andy Lloyd for *The Kundalini Serpent* and Tim Wallace-Murphy and Marilyn Hopkins for *Rosslyn*.

THE DREAMSTATE

The dreamstate, psychic experience that permeates our inner sanctum.

ROSSLYN

Pure white fantailed doves like seraphs fluttered in and out of the pine trees which stretched majestically above the facade and rooftops of the mansion. The name Rosslyn was carved (bas relief) in stone above the impressive portal. It was a haven and a retreat.

The date on the mantle showed 1666.

Numbers in ancient times.
The earth is carbon based.
The carbon atom comprises of:—6 negative charges (electrons); 6 positive charges (protons); 6 non-charged particles (neutrons).
The 666 appears in the Bible.
Here is wisdom let him
That has understanding count
The number of the beast
For it is the number of a man
And his number is 666

Revelation XIII, 18

9 is the highest number that can be reached before becoming one with God as in 10.

999 This represents Heaven above.
God, the soul or super God—a spiritual teacher
666 represents the earth (below)
Hell or the devil.
The purpose of life is to convert the 666 into Godly energy
999 (Enlightenment).
So it is written and is the science of the universe.

A GHOST STORY—THE HAUNTING

Tony Barrington, a university student, was taking time out from his music degree and was home for the half-term. Tony was brave, honest, and without superstition but a night he had at his seventeenth century family home was one he didn't forget too easily. The ghost stories he had heard from childhood were never founded and there were no facts or theories to prove otherwise.

It was late October 2009, the wind howled through the half naked trees, the golden leaves fluttered at his feet—it was the twilight hours when Tony arrived home. A dark cloud covered the silvery moon. He entered the house; a coldness made him shiver. He closed the door behind him and made his way into the living room. He poured himself a drink from the cabinet and settled down on the settee for some light reading.

The book he had chosen from the shelf spelt out the words *Ghosts and Ghouls*. He was just on page two when a scream of horror pierced his brain.

His mother shrieked his name again and again until he reached the top of the stairs. Fear and sweat masked his face. His fingers felt for the light switch; he flicked the switch on and off but there was no sign of light. Again, his fear grew.

He edged his way forward, then the light bulbs flickered on and off intermittently on their own. It was like the whole world had gone crazy.

He heard his name being called out again and again, only this time it was like ten or twelve people chanting all at once.

His panic was at its maximum.

"Tony, Tony. Tony."

Unceasingly, the chant continued until he reached his mother's bedroom. He stepped inside; the moonlight barely broke the darkness. Tony looked up in horror, an unbelievable sight rocked him back on his heels. The door slammed shut behind him. His mother's body hung in limbo ten feet above the bed, it began to circle the room in a slow horrifying manner.

Tony's blood drained from the surface of his body. His face was pure white; he shook his head violently, trying to gain some sanity about the passing few minutes.

He looked again and the floating body dropped to the floor with a sickening thud, its limbs twisted and broken.

Tony's face twitched, his eyes were like saucers as he stared in horror. His knees buckled under his fragile weight. He reached out to his loving mother. Kneeling by her side, he touched her cold, horrified face with the back of his hand. Suddenly, the light started to flicker as before. Yet another inhuman shrill filled the house. It sounded like it had come from Luke's room. Tony was in agony at leaving his mother but he knew Luke must be in danger.

His courage mounted and his fear subsided. He grabbed for the handle of the door. With all his force he wrenched it back and forth, pushed and pulled with all his might, but to no avail. His fists slammed against the woodwork in fury, still the screams rang in his ears, again the chant filled the air.

"Tony, Tony, Tony,"

His mind raced, a demented laughter joined in the devilish chorus. As he stepped back, the door flung open. A brilliant smoky light lit up the opening. Tony ran towards it without fear, without any thought of danger to himself. His only thought was for the safety of Luke.

He reached Luke's room. The door was open. He stepped inside tentatively, the light still flickered on and off in tormenting terror. The windows were flung open, the curtains fluttered in the cold breeze. Tony moved forward towards the gaping space. His eyes passed over the sill of the window and an even more horrific sight froze him to the Core.

The Young lifeless body of his brother Luke was impaled on the rusty iron fencing below. A spike was driven clean through his heart, the blood was dripping down his arms and onto the dirt below. Tony became light-headed. His mind could not grasp the intensity Of the nightmare he was undergoing. In an instant, Tony was elevated up and into the air as if catapulted by an invisible force. He landed the other side of the room, slamming sickeningly against the adjacent wall. He clambered to his feet, ignoring the pain to his head and back. He was in a daze, but could still focus on all that was happening. He staggered to the door.

A group of ghostly figures met his gaze, they beckoned him to Come with them, waving their arms, tempting and taunting, prodding and pushing him towards the bathroom.

The door swung open, his system was now immune to any shock that might marry itself to him.

Again, the laughter began as the apparitions faded away behind him. He moved solemnly, like a zombie awaiting the outcome of the next chapter to unfold in this hellish nightmare. He drew closer, the taps were running. The water lapped the edges of the bath, spilling out onto the bathroom floor. Tony looked down into the clear crystal water. The ashen face of his father stared up at him from beneath the watery depths. Bubbles popped the surface and the last gasp of breath ebbed away from his father's body. Tony reached in and pulled his father from the bath. He let out a cry of pain, like a dog howling at the moon. Again, his name was called out.

"Tony, Tony, Tony."

He rose to his feet, turned and walked down the hall towards the top of the stairs. He looked down the winding staircase and there the ghostly apparitions had assembled themselves. The ghouls were vile and ugly. Some had warts on their faces, their teeth were black and bloodridden. Their hands were bony; the nails were long and razor sharp. They giggled and laughed and chattered incessantly. They appeared to glow. They had no feet, their long grey and pinkish gowns wavered like chiffon in a breeze.

They beckoned him closer, taunting him again, pointing fingers, tempting him to come closer. Tony wondered what was in store for him—maybe a death like his mother broken limbs, slaughtered like his brother, impaled on the 'railings, or like his father, drowned beneath the water. At this moment he thought he was entering hell. They beckoned him; pointing fingers, laughing, snarling, sneering, teasing him, beckoning him to come to his fate—a fate he didn't know. it was his turn to be slaughtered, maimed or taken to hell in some unmerciful way. He slowly started down the stairs a step at a time.

They started their evil chants, their eyes blazed. Nothing was going to get Tony out of this mess, nothing was going to save him. Surely it was the end. They started chanting all in unison,

"Tony, Tony, Tony. Tony, come to us, come to us. Tony, Tony, Tony."

Luke grabbed Tony by the shoulders and shook him, "Tony, Tony, wake up, wake up, it's me."

Tony heard the thud of suitcases in the hallway.

We're home, we're home," Luke said again, Wake up, we're home."

Tony stood up, the book fell from his knee and onto the floor.

Tony hugged Luke,

"Oh, am I glad to see you!" he exclaimed.

Just then his father and mother entered the living room.

"Hi!"

His family had arrived home from holiday. Tony went and hugged his mother and father.

"Oh, what a dream, what a dream," he kept saying. "Oh, this is great, I love you all," he said.

"I'll put the kettle on," said his mother, "and we'll have a good chat about the holiday and how you've been getting on at university."

"Oh, you don't know the half of it!" muttered Tony.

They eventually retired to bed. On the way up the stairs Tony and Luke were arm in arm. Luke hesitated at the top of the stairway,

"Tony, tell me some ghost stories about the house,"

"No, Luke, maybe tomorrow. Goodnight."

FOR GOD
AND
GLORY

INVISIBLE SPIRIT

If you want to find God or the Divine, if you want to believe in a higher degree, if you need to be blessed with enlightenment, then look inside, inside yourself, have a goal. But have a purpose, a healthy purpose, for happiness and contentment. Settlement in the heart.

To care, to love, it's not a sacrifice. Have fun, build a future. Have patience and virtue. Keep an extra thought for Heaven, for goodness to consolidate your feelings. Have the strength to make a vow, to give yourself to yourself, the act of knowing "Self Generation". To resemble the will, the force and the truth of nature and faith in the invisible spirit, that resides in the heart and soul. That leap of faith, your own being within the manifestation of heavenly powers. The knowledge of infinite hope and glory and you will never be alone or in fear or dread. Keep a conviction, a reliance, a resolution, a resolve with courage and fortitude in the all encompassing abode of God.

THE HAUNTING

Tony awoke next morning still with the horrors of the night before churning in his mind. Although only a dream, it had its effect. He made his way to the bathroom, the October sun glinted through the chink in the sumptuous blue velvet curtains. He glared at himself in the mirror, his handsome features and glossy raven black hair gave him that Adonis look and appearance. His dark sultry almond brown eyes sparkled beyond measure. The high cheek bones like hewn granite held the structure of his stunning face. A strong chin set the personification of a screen idol. His teeth a perfection of ivory, shone through lips of burnt sienna, quite sensual for the male of the species. Fine, toned muscles rippled as he rested his arms against the rim of the basin. A slight foliage of dark hair spread itself across his bare chest. He was a lithe figure, 5ft 11in athletic and robust with a raw energy that kept him on his toes. A nervous energy that would exhaust another human body.

His loins were of ample proportion and superbly assembled with precision. He was uncircumcised and liked it that way. He especially liked the way girls drew back his foreskin before the onset of oral sex. As a blue beard and sexual predator Tony was one of the best in his category and was a lover of many. Five in all at the present moment in time. And there was more available if he ever ran short. Hordes in fact. Students from his university vied for his affection day and night. Gooey, glassy-eyed girls who would go down on their knees and pleasure him at the drop of a hat, or a raise on his eyebrow, or a wave of his hand, abandoning all inhibitions in order to please him, waiting for that contented smile of his. He could also go like a stud for lengthy periods as it took him quite a while to arrive at a climax. A thing he never really understood. But the ladies were happy with the scenario, sometimes climaxing themselves two or three times in process. There was no time for sentiment in Tony's life. It was one long constantly motivated escapade through the cosmological order of things. The ladies were top priority, but his music came first. Music was in his soul. The females, the sex, that was just part of living.

Although a lethario, he had a heart of gold. There was a Jesus element about him. Some people said he had a heart as big as a mountain. He loved children and disliked injustice. His love could be overwhelming. He would sweep people off their feet with his unabounding love and tenderness. A touch of his hand could calm and baby's cry and he could generate a feeling of calmness in a raucous crowd. His family ached if he was away for long periods. Luke, his younger brother, looked on him as a god. A unique unbridled fortification of security which rested his soul and helped him sleep at night. Tony re-emerged from the bathroom and on to the small landing area leading to the adjacent bedrooms, six in all.

The main bedroom was mum and dad's. The smallest (but most adequate) was Luke's. The one Tony held was a luxurious utility unit with a mini gym, a shower, hand basin and a loo for "emergencies". In another section was a studio with an eight track consul, guitar stand and PA system, stool and music stand. His bed was king size with satin sheets and giant pillows of duck-down. A spacious walk-in wardrobe and dressing area was three feet away. To the right was a writing desk, his pride and joy. Topped with a blue leather trim which was decorated with ornate gold edging. It was a rare find, unearthed in an antique shop near to his home. He'd searched for months for the right one, and there it was, on his doorstep. Solid mahogany and in pristine condition. A giant mirror flanked a large panelled area where fluffy chocolate coloured towels hung on the chrome heated rails which eminated from the heating system. Tony stood and watched as Luke wandered down the hall rubbing his eyes with his knuckles, wavering from side to side, sleepy eyed and indifferent.

"Careful sleepy head! Watch were yer goin!" Tony exclaimed fluffing his hair with his outstretched hand as he passed him by. A face towel was slung over his bare shoulder. "Wakey! wakey!", he announced again. "Come on, me 'n' you outside now! Let's see what you got!" Tony put his fists up as a prize fighter would do ready for battle. "Queensberry rules now! Come on!". Tony was dancing on tip toes, jabbing southpaw style. Luke's arms dropped to their sides, his shoulders limp and listing forward, looked in disbelief at Tony's antics. A Mona Lisa smile was ready to burst into an enormous grin full of happiness and laughter. "Arhh!" Tony exclaimed again. "Forget it! You got no chance anyway! See ya later!" he proffered.

The house was massive, sitting proudly on the Wirral peninsular. Looking out across Liverpool Bay scanning the Welsh hills, one could encapsulate the glory and symmetry of the north of England, Wales and the facade of Merseyside. That great rock 'n' roll city. In fact, a world in one city. Beatle land. The source of all humour and unquestionable talent. But his Wirral was more subdued, more remote, more sedate, more alien to the conventional masses of Merseyside. Some days and nights it could be so bleak. Although a place of beauty and pleasant countryside, it had a malevolence that gave one tremors and chilled the blood. A mist could descend within seconds clouding the house in its four acres of land, its pathway obscured from view was a little on an incline and winding through a thick copse of wooded area. A white gravel causeway snaked a path to a fountain and main door of the house. The fountain was massive with a statue of Eros at its centre, spouting a spray of water from its mouth down a set of black stone steps rippling the moat below as it cascaded down. A serene calming affect that relaxed any visitor on sight. It was heavenly at times, when the sun shone in the summer months.

Tony's Romany roots came from his mother. A ravishing beauty of immense stature. Eloquent and sophisticated in the late seventies, she adorned the covers of fashion magazines of the day and graced the catwalks of many fashion houses. Art and design was her forte and a lucrative business in dressmaking which made her independent and fulfilled. Working from home she could combine family life and the pursuits of labour with comfort and pleasure. Her strawberry blonde hair would swirl and flow over her shoulders in a flurry like gossamer as she sashayed along corridors and halls within the house. Multi-coloured ribbons and silks and fabrics of different makes draped over her arms, pins clenched between the teeth of her sensuous mouth, eyes flashing with the invention of her next artistic endeavour. Sweeping the glorious open stairways in anticipation of a new client when the doorbell rang and an appointment was scheduled. Of course, there was a seamstress when the work load became too much for one person. There was also a housekeeper who worked daily, or when there was a large dinner party or an event at the mansion, the Romany connection came through the family tree, passed down from great grandparents and relatives from the Forest of Dean in 16th Century Gloucestershire when the nomads arriving in Britain called themselves 'The Dukes of little Egypt', hence the name 'gypsies', named by her grandmother (a fortune teller) Rosa St Clare, became Rosa Barrington, marrying Glen Barrington after a whirlwind romance.

Glen Barrington's roots ebbed back to Scotland. His father a Scottish Laird was renowned through the Highlands and Lowlands as a true and just man his wealth was accumulated through the sale of cattle, buying and selling, breeding and marketing for the locality. His father before him herded cattle through the Glens and his father before him rubbed shoulders with the famous Rob Roy 1671-1734 cattle freebooter, rustler and protector for the local gentry. A somewhat dubious but profitable occupation. The family buying the English retreat as a staging post for English and Welsh business transaction. Glen, being the eldest son, took up residence in the year of '77 when his father past away. His mother, now a Scottish widow moved back to the Scottish ancestral home the same year.

The family assets were now firmly set and secured through with financial institutions, stocks and shares were the big thing in the '70s and '80s. Money was well invested in New York, Hong Kong and Scotland, England and Wales. Conglomerates, corporations and financial houses were now the structure of business that Glen Barrington had to deal with on a daily basis. The Barringtons always sat down to dinner together whenever possible, of course, Rosa, a great cook, would be in the enormous country style kitchen. Preparing favourite meals for the boys and her man. Nothing was too good for those she eternally loved so well. Glen was a stickler for routine and healthy appetites and family gatherings, chatting and discussing the day's events with his family around him. After dinner, coffee was served in the lounge and he would ask how the boys were doing. Luke was 17, doing his A levels and would soon be moving to University to study medicine. Tony was already an accomplished musician and writer and had a novel and two CD albums to his credit. A black belt 1st dan in Ju-Jitsu and had boxed for the local youth club in the area, gaining a couple of trophies in the process. His three year music course at Liverpool University was coming to an end and his efforts were being noticed by the fraternity 'therein'. He was making progress in leaps and bounds. Luke's pastime was his doves. He bred them and cared for them since he was 15 years old, securing a dovecote at the rear of the house for his own personal pleasure, a "stress buster", and a time out from his studies and school work. His pride and joy, some were worth up to £500. He would endlessly watch as they flew in grand swooping circles over and above the houses and shoreline of the River Mersey. They were his home birds and his treasured possessions. Sitting cross legged by the open log fire while Tony usually always stood (his restfulness always showed through), Luke listened to his father's advice when he would lecture the boys on behaviour and standards. Looking up at Tony for confirmation as Dad methodically chattered on and one in sermon-like fashion. But his young sons adored their father, and idolised their mother.

Glen Barrington was tall, 6ft 2in, a fit active man, tennis and golf his favourite pastimes. Black thick set hair with a touch of silver grey at the temples swept itself back from his broad forehead and hooded, dark eyes in waves and kiss curls. The bagpipes were his special talent and Christmas time would see them emerge from the attic in time for Hogmanay. He was a lithe figure with a slight paunch. The days of full physical fitness was not quite the order of the day now that he was retired and comfortable with his lifestyle a country gent I suppose. As captain in the Scots Guard, he was now on a pension and glad to be out of his tour of duty and could get on with the family concerns. Glen gave readily to charity and organisations dedicated to the NSPCC. A solid citizen, albeit rich and accomplished in all manner of affluence. Rich and famous, I guess. As with his dazzling wife a couple renowned and respected.

Tony now in his mid 20's was expected to carry the Barrington traditions and would do so with astonishing success. Luke had his mother's looks. The blonde hair had a hint of shadow that gave it an unusual colour. His pearl grey eyes were his mothers but everything else spoke of his father. A much more genteel delicate nature shone through. Thoughtful, concise and controlled. A good addition to the human race. A humane being for all mankind.

Tony's next thought was breakfast. Luke had cleaned up and was heading for the dovecot to check the birds, give them their morning feed and change their drinking water. Rosa was making glen's favourite breakfast meal, scrambled eggs and smoked salmon with black pepper, honey, crispy toast, pure orange juice, iced water and coffee with cream. Gerta, the housemaid was laying the table. Tony was glad to be home, away from the halls of residence where things were a little "studenty" if you get the meaning. He liked his fellow students but loved the affection and care he received at home. Plus he was surrounded by his precious instruments and with his writing desk and gym he was in his own element creative and awe-inspiring. Like Alexander the Great! Only not so reckless and bloodthirsty. The music business was what he wanted to conquer. His poetry was unique, exotic, glorifying, profound, romantic, first poetry, then song writing. Poetry in motion, as they say. His development grew over the years from arduous practice night and day. His fingers at times were left calloused and near to bleeding. No pain, no gain is the saying, and creativity is a wondrous thing.

"Tony's breakfast". Freshly squeezed orange juice to start. Porridge drizzled with honey and little cream to give it that rich texture. Three eggs (free range) cooked in butter over a gentle gas, with thinly sliced beef tomatoes fanned around the edge of the plate, and a slice of fried bread cut in triangles neatly placed at right angles. He like the crunch of the fried bread with his morning feast, it gave him an edge. The crunchiness echoing through his senses. The delicious taste of the repast tempting his taste buds. Breakfast was important to him. There was something about breakfast. It opened up a new day. It summoned the new dawn. A new pleasure, a new challenge. A springboard for creative endeavours. The starting pistol for the race, hurdles, sprint or marathon.

Luke was different. Food wasn't an issue, it was a chore. Anything would do as long as it was put in front of him. He would gladly sit with his doves and share their 'corn'. As for items on the menu he was indifferent, in fact inconsequential, to the frustration of Rosa and Gerta, standing hands on hips, and then scratching one's head. Teenagers "eh"! Rosa's grapefruit was an ever present item. The first thing on the breakfast table, eight o'clock on the dot. There it would be segmented with artistry, sitting glorious and majestic in it's crystal glass coupe. A petite silver spoon and fork poised at the sides. A statement of sovereign rule. A precursor for the "regal" entrance of its owner. "Rosa" the matriarch. That grapefruit was a mark of distinction, a clarification of authority, control and supremacy. But of course, in the nicest possible and motherly way. Silver napkin rings with the Barrington name and crest emblazoned in bas relief added the finishing touch to the perfectly laid grandiose oak table. Breakfast over!

"Just toast for Luke and a glass of milk. The family went their special ways. Gerta was left with the drudgery, but she enjoyed her work. Tony was already back in his room and strumming away with his newly acquired Taylor. A magnificent guitar, financed by Mum and Dad from his inheritance which would be his on the 22nd May 2014, his thirtieth birthday. When he had accomplished all he desired and his parents were satisfied with his efforts to get an education and become a responsible adult and man of the world and of society. Money and status would be in better hands at that moment in time. Rosa busied herself as usual in the annexe, her workshop and study. Glen had meetings on Merseyside. Property development hand land leasing were uppermost this month, October 2009. The financial climate was a bit shaky but things would pick up, he was certain of that. Luke also took to his room for last minute studies, before he was back at school. The prime objective were his biology and chemistry exams. A's were vitally important to his cause wanting to be a chemist or doctor, he was in it for the long haul. But he had the initiative and guile to succeed. Game boys and Ipods seemed to be the two components of Luke's world. Oh! And paintballing whenever the moment struck him, a quick phone call to school friends could set up the escapade. Verbal communication with adults was never instigated except in emergencies, or to gain an answer to a riddle, or receive financial support for a sojourn, or to entreat for all the latest gadgets and gizmos on the market. And then there was the latest style get up all the rest of the boys wore. That was important beyond belief.

Teenagers eh! Then there were girls. "Mmmm . . . . not quite there just yet. Let's get some grades first", he thought 'Clever boy'. That he was.

Tony had this psychic element to his personality. He could feel things, he was alert to fundamental occurrences. Like things when people were under stress, or ill, or in a situation of foreboding, mostly relatives, friends, associates. Sometimes if the phone rang, he would have a name in his head, or a feeling of situations that may occur. Many a time he'd seen the future. When the déjà vu would be so strong that he knew he had seen it all before, and the connection was so vivid that it had been a "vision" months before, sometimes years before. These omens he had learnt of over the years foretold of good fortune, or of times in his life that was to be consequential or important to his existence. But these moments were never to be of dread or fear. But an acceptance of time lines, and eras, and formations in the physical cycle of his rollercoaster journey through the cosmological order of things. The never-ending progress of the soul's esoteric path through eternity, within the human body. ESP, clairvoyance, telepathy, epiphany, the sixth sense, astral travel. The biological essence, sensations, interspersed, living, breeding. The primordial domination of active participation. "Theos" the God within.

But Tony was his own man. He would allow things into his world, he could accept the rigours of the day. He endured the idiosyncrasies, the twists, the turns, the confrontations, the dilemmas in the circus of life. Yet there was an instinctive inner process that held his equilibrium in place. A consciousness that pervaded through the order of things. A structure, a blue print for the future. A set of rules regulated, relived, encapsulated. Certain agendas gelling in the back of his mind offset the natural conforms of social activities. Tony was not one to converse over the fence too often. He didn't gossip. He could never court a mundane existence such as that. Living in general was too precious, to be so boring.

Tony wasn't a great drinker. He liked a few beers with friends. Students were great athletes in that pass time, he had learnt. He liked a glass of rose wine from time to time. But when it came to spirits, well, he would rather be in control of his life. Spirits tended to make him a bit outlandish if Tony had had one or two too many. The congregation would soon know about it. He was funny and a life and soul of the party, singing and dancing with great affection, sometimes a little over the top. But that was Tony. People loved him for it (if the truth be known).

He had a natural singing voice. His dulcet tones could be heard (on occasion) around the house when he would hum and sing some refrain he was learning. Or he would try out one of his new compositions, the melody and lyrics ringing out from his bedroom window, filling the country air around the compounds of the estate. Some local open mike nights welcomed him with open arms. People would sing out loud the choruses to some of his songs. A sign in itself that he had a nucleus of fans that appreciated his music.

Tony had been playing chords for a full hour, his fingers were numb and his hand ached. But the music at times was good, some new songs were coming through the ether and into his mind. Masturbation wasn't a big thing in Tony's life. He'd rather have some pretty maid perform the act for him and he reminded himself it had been quite a while since "you know what". He should move things on and quickly. A phone call or two was in the thought process, or maybe his testosterone was speaking for itself. Many a time the phone had rang and there was a female acquaintance on the other end, looking to chat? "What a guy". Things were quiet that winter, and Tony was courting one of his conquests on a regular basis. This was an unusual turn of events. They were like knots in a long piece of string. But this knot was one he particularly lingered on. Annette was different, steady, alluring. Things fitted right, there was a surrendering quality in her loving "Venus's fly trap" maybe. Would she change his world? Would she be the rock he needed? Would she be the sum of the parts to create the whole? Would she hold his hand and hug and kiss? Would she console and assure, or would she demand and question? Would she intrude and spoil? Would she condemn or abuse? But there was a love, there was a connection. A mutual adherence. An unforeseen spectre possibly? Fate, destiny, predestination, divine will? It's in the stars, the wrath of Mars, the celestial sphere, heavenly hum, the fortunes of life that's yet to come.

Annette was an attractive girl, with dark auburn coloured hair. Her eyes were a deep brown, round, bright and open. Enamel white teeth with an enchanting irregular angle reflected a sallow opaque skin. A little like Greek or Egyptian in looks. She was a size twelve, so a little chunky but womanly curvy. Tony like this kind of female.

Skinny, dizzy blondes never really did it for him but he would never turn away the chance of a liaison d'amour. Sex was sex, women were women. Annette was afraid of changing Tony's lifestyle, and knew of his promiscuous casanova ways but she felt there was a gentleman and a good heart in the midst of it all. People in their twenties, teenagers, they lived this life of promiscuity but love would conquer. The cinema, the restaurants, days out, drinks at the local, maybe a show at the theatre. It was a courtship but not too intense. Holding hands, strolling arm in arm, kissing on the doorsteps, a romantic weekend away. There was a bond, a tender attachment. Annette understood that Tony was a free spirit.

Love making with Annette at first was one of a one night stand mode. Tony was a free agent regarding who he brought home and who he didn't bring home. It was usually late and conducted within the confines of and privacy of his bedroom. Boozy nights and things of a sexual and flirtatious manner occurred at the halls of residence. Things like that were rife in that quarter of Merseyside and the Wirral. But there was not many lovers that Tony would invite into his home.

Annette was a little shy, a bit self conscious but also proud, timid and cautious. She did not like to hang around in the mornings in case she bumped into Tony's mum or dad. She would leave early or Tony would escort her home in a taxi or maybe walk her to her abode which was in the vicinity. She's had one or two lovers but was not the type to be lascivious. One thing that Tony adored was oral sex and foreplay. Kissing, touching, feeling, breasts were his preference but it all counted in lovemaking. Legs, buttocks, arms, shoulders, lips, the nape of the neck, hair, cheeks. The mouth "oh" the mouth, hot, full open, moist. The tongue, soft and tender dwelling in that sensuous cavity, not a small mouth but large and supple. At first Annette was reluctant to succumb to this aspect of love but Tony eventually cajoled her into something "I imagine" she enjoyed immensely. She was a lady and would conduct herself on her own terms but secretly loved Tony's passion and warmth and intensity. Sometimes Tony had to keep his ardour down as his bed might be head creaking through the walls of the mansion along with distinct cries of ecstasy. "What a guy". There's not many as romantic as Tony.

Romance was a big thing in his life. Flowers, chocolates, poetry. He would dish them all out when the moment was right. He cared for his lovers. One birthday present he bought Annette was a silky low-cut azure lacy nightgown. This was kept snugly folded in top draw. A hair brush, body spray, perfume. The odd trinket sat upon his dresser. He loved her to wear this item of clothing. It was so sleek against her fair skin. He loved her breasts so plump and ample. She was sultry and fleshy. Voluptuous and lusty, but not overly sexy, more demure. Sometimes Annette would shush Tony at times of passion afraid of being overheard. Tony's parents were very discreet, and never was there a word spoke disparagingly, or in jest.

Annette worked for a massive Law firm on the Wirral. As a secretary and sometimes personal assistant she frequented Court rooms and the Law Courts on occasions so she knew of the World and its ways. An intelligent girl with a law degree. But she would bide her time and gain experience before embarking on a grander scale. Her father was a bank manager, her mother a nurse. Her home was a detached cottage but nowhere on the degree and range of Tony's huge estate. She had four brothers, two sisters all younger than herself, so was in fact a little bit of a Mother hen to her siblings.

Glen and Rosa had the main bedroom which looked out onto the fountain and courtyard. Central and perched against a mirrored wall was a heart-shaped king size divan with 10 inch deep thick mattress for comfort and rest. A red satin overlay spread the length and breadth, gleaming like a gemstone against the lush deep turquoise carpet. Persian rugs sat nestling either side. Two more beds, double in size were against adjacent walls, both sides of the massive room. En-suite facilities were augmented alongside spacious walk-in wardrobes with push button controls. His and hers own bathroom, shower, toilet, vanity stand and wash basin. Assorted deep blue luxurious towels embossed with the name 'Rosa' and 'Glen' stacked the pine wood shelving. This was their boudoir, their love nest. The heart shaped bed, the communal loving place for the meeting of their hearts. For their unbridled love and devotion. A dedicated sanctity for the inviolate passion affection and joy. Naked and cleansed upon the sheet, caressing, vowing their love in carnal splendour. Pure unmitigating, unsullied, unbounding seraphic delight. They both had their worlds and coveted them as equally as each other. A self sanctifying agreement of unselfishness giving each other their precious space and time. But when they came together the adoration and amour knew no bounds.

It was a private area with an anteroom. There were locks on all the bedroom doors of the mansion. Discretion was top priority. Security was vital in their world. Embarrassment and unforeseen circumstances never presented themselves. Luke and Tony would never think of intruding on their personal level (their inner most personal retreat). If Tony or Luke ever needed to speak to their parents or seek Glen or Rosas whereabouts they would always knock and wait at the entrance of "that" sanctuary. There was an intercom, for late night disturbances, which resounded with a symphony of chimes through the grand chamber.

Rosa would appear gracefully, close the doors behind here and enquire as to what was needed, or who wished to speak to her, then would direct matters elsewhere, to the study or lounge. Close family would be asked into the foyer where a large lampshade stood against a chaise-longue. A small drop leaf writing desk with pen and note pad sat in a small alcove. Sliding doors concealed the main sleeping section in return Mum or Dad would always knock on Tony's or Luke's room. Gerta always knocked and waited at all doors.

SEX

ex is the most basic instinct there. There's a saying (behind closed doors), private affairs, personal feelings, loving tenders, naked thrust, naked love, sensuous moments, erotic liaisons, the freedom of speech. Inhibitions discarded, set free. Emotions fulfilled, healed and soothed. Sexual healing. Responses to natural understanding. Caresses, affections love. Sex yes, but love, always. Sex without love is lust, lust is a sin. Rosa and Glen (loved) their love was all-consuming, complete. No embarrassment, no restrictions. Permission is a beautiful thing. Carnal knowledge of each other's erogenous zones. Rosa and Glen knew each other's so well. A look, a touch would be the requisite for their meeting of the hearts. There were moments of mutual affection, foreplay, light playful frisky times when they would tickle and tempt. Glen would catch her at the table or in the kitchen when he would see her kneading the dough or soaked in suds, elbows deep. He would glide in behind her with hands around her waist using his palms to massage and caress the ventral area below her breasts. He would kiss the nape of her neck. She always coiffured her hair in a French pleat when she was working in the kitchen. Tingles would reverberate through her body, waking the sensations and re-tuning the receptors in her nervous system. She would raise her head and rest it on his shoulder wishing it was a better time or place. He would leave her and return to his obligations and the business at hand. She would glance a look his way, catch his eye and smile ever so knowingly.

When they loved, it was a tender explosion. They would be naked, essence of lavender would permeate the air, oils would burn, candles would flicker. Perfumes and fragrances, incense, eau de cologne, pot pourri swamped their senses. Pomade for Rosa's hair, which gleamed and shone like golden threads over her shoulders and glorious breasts. Her body slightly talced, smooth and even to the touch. The cleansing of their bodies was a ritual, clinical and regulated. Their toilet duties second to none. Nothing got in the way of their sacred loving. They would meet, he would hold her hand lightly in his kissing her open mouth feeling the gentle vacuum of her breath, the temptation galloping in his heart and pulse. He would caress and linger on those lips, enjoying their heat and taste and tingling sensation. His manhood now aroused, solid and moist. She would rest her soft manicured hands upon his hips, feeling his buttocks, so firm and manly. Her deep crimson coloured nails digging into his hot flesh, guiding them down and up against his huge testicles, massaging them gently, feeling his eight inch penis in her hand, fondling it. This was her comforter, her own property, her possession. It was almost part of her anatomy.

No time to waste, she was there down on her knees. She knew Glen loved this. The sucking, the kissing. Holding on to his muscled leg for balance, she would flick her hair back and take his colossal, full erect member between her ruby lips and into her tempting mouth. Her eyes flashing up at Glen with joyous abandon. Those eyes bewitching, sexy. The delicately applied make up accentuating her looks for maximum pleasure. Glen, gazing at her mouth full with this pulsating penis, sheer ecstasy, he thought. She would massage and stroke his shaft slowly and deliberately. He would raise her from the floor and guide her to the bed. She would lick her lips in delight of the act. Readying herself for the next onset of more pleasure, legs splayed open, showing her full, splendid glory, soft and moistured by the foreplay. Head arched back resting on her forearms, her hair hanging loose waiting for Glen to weave his magic. First he would take time to kiss her inner thighs. He loved her slender, adorable legs, smooth and delicate, he would bite and nip at the supple, yielding flesh. Then the deep, meaningful exploration, his tongue would penetrate well beyond the vestibule over the regions of her clitoris and labia, sending her into blissful realms of euphoria. Then back to her breasts, still kissing her hot body running his hands over her raised nipples covering them with his fiery breath, licking and fondling with his tongue endlessly back and forth from one to the other, squeezing gently like a new born to its mother. Then, his steaming piston-like rod like a torpedo homing in on its expected target would guide itself into the opening. A helping hand by Glen for a soft entry, tickling the entrance to her vagina with the head of his massive organ, the thrust even and sure of its path to her inner sanctum. She would grasp the soft billowy cushions that lay about her, writhing in sheer lustful wantoness. Wrapping her legs around his waist to gain more of his body against hers, feeling him insider her, she would buck like a mule, jerking, thrusting her pelvis against his. Glen would drive forward, pumping vigorously holding her buttocks, gaining full penetration, perspiration clinging to every part of their anatomies. It was time Glen was about to explode, his semen like molten lava was about to erupt and Rosa knew it. In her passion she wanted it all. She wanted to savour the moment. She wanted the wholepackage. She wanted to be fulfilled. She had climaxed but needed to be complete. Glen was ready, his face contorted in delight. Rosa was in a trance, the thrill of it all was rapturous. She eased Glen away from her, taking his erupting penis, smothering it with her lips. Glen burst forth. Rosa held firm, taking his semen full in her mouth savouring every last drop until he was dry and overwhelmed with the thrill of it. They embraced, cheek to cheek, touching, caressing, still the extant tremors vibrated through their systems. Trembling, they fell to the palms like velvet dolls on a cloud. Serenity, the seraphic, the divine, the heavenly encounter they always knew was theirs and theirs alone.

Rosa, in one of her mother hen modes would seek out her boys before retiring, with two mugs of cocoa on a silver tray. Knocking gently hoping to wish them goodnight, Luke would answer his bedroom door. Tight lipped and pleased with herself "Cocoa is the best thing for you" she would pronounce every time. She's so funny, Luke thought, looking at her like she was an angel caught in the bathing white light of an incandescent glow.

She would move on to Tony's room. He would invite her in, glad of her presence. He would sometimes play her his latest tune. This was one he particularly liked. "Listen to this mum" he would say. She would put the tray on the nearest resting place and consider the music. As Tony sat on his bed with the guitar in his lap he would strum softly, (this one was a melodic ballad). "It's rainin, it's rainin, dark clouds up above, it's rainin, it's rainin, thinking about your love" he sang. Looking to her for her appeal and comments, she would listen, head slightly at an angle trying to hear the melody. Appearing appreciative as possible, straightening the lapels of her chunky woollen housecoat, retying the belt nervously. "That's very good dear, you keep that up. That is a very nice song". She would kiss his forehead "Now sleep well and drink your cocoa". She would say with an angelic smile as she would close the door over very gently. "Mum" Tony would whisper almost out loud and smile shaking his head quizingly, but with so much love in his heart.

There's a natural advancement to living but there's also thought control. A continuity to maintain the leverage needed for peace and tranquility, to harness a will to succeed, to honour the righteousness within. To harmonise with the relevant courses of mankind. To be free to indulge without fear or retribution. To believe to sustain. There's a god given power for you to employ with meaningfulness, with love. To endeavour to triumph without guilt or pain without anxiety. To manipulate the structure of nature into a celebration of good will and generosity. To be a good Samaritan (within reason) with a strategy for hope and integrity in an endearing world. To refine, to equate yourself to a resolution to believe, and you will see.

To knock and the door will open. To ask and you will receive. To seek and you will find.

Our story is one of horror but the Wirral has the gift of pleasurable countryside. There's a different element to its rustic charm, it's clean and unhindered. It has a link to North Wales and this gives it a feel of grace although rural in a sense, it has its industrial areas and rural parts but in effect it's charming and has some of the most enchanting villages and sites of historic value, not hard like some inner cities, but gentle in style. It breathes a healthy atmosphere. Some names to conjure up Hoylake, New Brighton, Neston, Heswall, pleasant graceful towns with tree lined avenues and glorious view out onto the River Dee, the Welsh hills and its coast line.

Come away from the ongoing saga of the Barringtons, I would like to take you on an excursion around this part of the country with a little history and factual data, away from the gruesome events which infiltrate this world.

SANCTUARY IN THE SEA

The Wirral Peninsula is situated between two major rivers. To the east the Mersey, which rises in the distant Pennines as a pure, sparkling stream, but during its course through industrial Lancashire becomes increasingly polluted until, by the time it flows through the narrow channel twixt the ports of Birkenhead and Liverpool, its waters are muddy-hued. The Dee, on the other hand, rises in the Welsh uplands and, twisting its way across open moorland and wooded valleys, makes its way through the city of Chester and across the broad sands between Wales and Wirral, to empty its untainted waters into the Irish Sea.

If the two rivers are so different, then so too are their estuaries. That of the Mersey is narrow, barely a mile across, its banks lined with cranes and wharves of Liverpool's dockland. The estuary of the Dee is wide, five miles from Red Rocks on the Wirral side to Point of Ayr on the Welsh side; its backcloth the hill and peaks of North Wales, it sands and channels the haunt of birds and seals.

Here is a "surviving wilderness", a sanctuary for wildlife of every description, where the only sounds are the lonely cries of curlew and oyster-catcher, the moaning of the seals and the rushing of the tide. A beautiful area at all times of the year: in summer, when the setting sun casts rainbow colours across the ebbing waters; or in winter, when the wind churns the waters of the estuary into a foaming, churning cauldron. And always, the mysterious hills and mountains are an every-changing backcloth to the waters and sands of the estuary; sometimes dark and brooding under a glowering November sky; often a green patchwork of fields and hedgerows in summer; and occasionally capped with snow on a January day.

The peace and solitude to be found in the estuary belies its history. For this was the gateway to Chester for over 1,700 years, a period which began with the Romans and their troopships, and ended with the seventeenth-century traders desperately trying to keep alive the anchorages along Wirral's Deeside in competition with burgeoning Liverpool. The ghost-quays of Dawpool, Gayton and Neston still stand as reminders of those long-forgotten trading days when ships from the Baltic, Ireland, France, Spain, Portugal, and the Low Countries plied these waters.

The trading ships left, and the Dee with its estuary was left to the local fishermen and the sea birds. Even the twentieth century has had little impact. Fortunately so, for the Dee estuary is now officially recognised as being of international importance for the wading birds which winter here in their tens of thousands. Each autumn, about three million waders leave their breeding grounds in the Arctic to spend the winter on the estuaries of Europe and north-west Africa; of these, some 150,000 come to the Dee, making it one of the four most important sites in Britain.

The birds are attracted by the fifty or so square miles of sand and mud which are exposed at low tide, and which harbour an abundance of marine life. Some forty thousand or more, feed in the mudflats of the estuary during a typical winter. Oyster-catchers, whose total numbers often exceed twenty thousand, sit out the high tide in their favourite mudflat haunts as the tide recedes. Redshank, turnstone, curlew, purple sandpiper all winter here in large numbers.

The concentration of winter birds in the estuary is not generally noticeable at low tide; but as the water rises, so the birds are forced off the mud and sand to the rocks, islets and the margins of the estuary. As the feeding grounds are covered by the tide, so flock after flock rises, performing mass aerobatics, their colours alternating black and white against the sea and sky. Suddenly the birds, as if with a single corporate eye, will spot a suitable patch of sand or rock and drop to the ground with on accord.

During spring and autumn, huge numbers of passing migrants use the estuary to feed and rest during their long flights between Africa and the Arctic. In spring ringed plover, sanderling and dunlin pause here briefly *en route* to Greenland where they breed during the short Arctic summer. During autumn the estuary is a global cross-roads; returning spring migrants feed alongside oyster-catchers from Scotland, bar-tailed godwits from Russia, and knot from the Arctic.

The summer months are the quietest for bird life, although the arrival of the terns in the spring—sandwich, common, Arctic and little—makes up for the reduced numbers of wading birds.

The estuary's greatest attraction, the Hilbre Islands, are situated right at the mouth of the estuary, where the waters of the Dee meet the Irish Sea. Here is a group of islands, accessible on foot twice a day, with a charm and fascination found nowhere on the mainland. On these islands it is possible to experience that sense of isolation and remoteness rarely found in modern living; especially so close to a large centre of population.

The Hilbre Islands are about a mile and a half off the north-western tip of the peninsula, and consist of Hilbre itself (12 acres), Middle Hilbre (3 acres), and Little Eye (1/2 acre). The two larger islands are only a few hundred yards apart; but Little Eye is almost a mile from the main pair. All three are connected by a strip of sandstone reef intersected by countless channels and rock pools.

It seems certain that the islands were originally much larger than their present size, and possibly joined together as one. It is know, for example, that in the middle of the sixteenth century, some 4,000 foot and horse troops camped here on their way to Ireland—an impossibility today. Early maps of Cheshire show the Hilbre group as a single island; and it seems likely that the islands were at one time part of the mainland. Geologically speaking, such rapid changes in so short a time span would seem unlikely unless seen against the nature of the rock and the local climatic conditions. Hilbre, like so much of Wirral is made up of the red-yellow Bunter sandstone; an extremely soft, crumbly stone which simply cannot stand up to the ferocious battering so common a feature of these western coasts. In fact, it is likely that, but for the extensive work carried out to reinforce the seaward-facing cliffs of the main island, it would have been almost cut in two by now.

There is so much to see on the Hilbre Islands; but first a short account of their fascinating past. In spite of their apparent remoteness, man has used the islands since very early times. Various finds indicate the presence of Stone Age and Bronze Age man. The Romans, too, used the islands; shards of third and fourth century pottery were found here in 1926. During the seventh century Hilbre was the home of one Hildeburgh, who chose this barren place to live out a solitary life of penance and prayer. The island owes its name to this good lady who was remembered long after her death. It seems likely that she became an almost legendary figure, for a shrine or chapel dedicated to St Hildeburgh was set up, and this became known as the Chapel of St Mary. Brownbill suggests that a small religious house had been founded on Hilbre, possibly before the Norsemen settled in the district in or about 905. Although this is not mentioned in the Doomsday Book, mention *is* made of the two churches of Chirceb (West Kirby): "One in the town and the other on an island in the sea near thereto." Before 1081 these churches belonged to the monks of St Evroul in Normandy, who later gave them to the Benedictine monks of St Werburgh's Abbey, Chester.

The monks of St Werburgh's established on Hilbre a small cell dedicated to the Virgin Mary. This island became a populat place for pilgrims during the thirteenth and fourteenth centuries; Holinshed, the famous chronicler of the time, remarked: "And thither went a sort of superstitious fools, in pilgrimage to our Lady of Hilbre, by whose offerings the monk there were cherished and maintained." No traces of the cell have been found, although a red sandstone cross said to be from the early church was found on the island in 1853. A 40-foot well, cut through the solid rock and commonly thought to have been sunk by the monks is more likely to have been made in the nineteenth century.

The monks lived out their lonely life on Hilbre until the middle of the sixteenth century. What an isolated existence it must have been for the two monks who "did their turn" here. Small wonder that legends have been woven around them. The sands between Hilbre and the North Wales coast are often referred to as the "Constable's Sands". About the year 1101 Richard, Earl of Chester, was on a peaceful pilgrimage to St Winifred's Shrine at Holywell when he was ambushed by "Wicked Welshmen". Richard sent world to his constable, William Fitz-Nigel of Halton, to raise a great army to meet him at Basingwerk. The constable and his men rode fast to Hilbre, hoping to find barques to take them across the estuary to Wales, but all the boats were out. Remembering the monks on the island, Fitz-Nigel asked them to pray to St Werburgh on behalf of his master, promising them a substantial gift on his way home. Instantly the deep waters of the estuary parted, and the constable and his men crossed over a bank of dry sand to the Welsh shore where he rescued the Earl and returned safely to Chester.

The last monk left the island about 1550, probably because Hilbre was becoming less of a sanctuary. In fact, by this time it had become a busy place as a shipping centre for vessels sailing to and from the port of Chester. the following extract from the Chester Customs Accounts for the year 1566 gives some indication of the volume of traffic trading between here and Ireland:

27th March: "George of Hilbre" (12 tons) owned by Thomas Mowely of Hilbre, to Dublin with 6 tons coal from Chester.

7th October: "John of Hilbre) (16 tons) owned by Richard Rathbone to Dublin with small wares—£4.

8th October: "Jesus of Hilbre" (14tons) owned by Thomas Queyntrie to Dublin, 2 pieces of Yorkshire Kersey, 1 piece of yellow western Kersey, ½ piece of western Kersey.

17th October: "Bride of Hilbre")24tons) owned by Thomas Queyntrie, to Dublin, 10 tons of coal.

27th March (1567): "Ellen of Hilbre" (12 tons) owned by Richard Rathbone of Hilbre to Dublin, 6 tons of coal.

Inwards to Chester

2nd April: "Sunday of Hilbre" (3 tons) owned by Williams Ratclyff, Kersey and 1 case white wooden cups value £8, 2 cases hops, ½ case aniseed, 12 case castle soap, 5 cases of trenchers of the common sort.

6th April: "Katherine of Hilbre" (16 tons) owned by John Androwe of West Kirby.
"Nicholas of Hilbre" (16 tons) owned by Thomas Ratclyff of Dublin, 3 cases of sheep fells, 4 cases of Brockfells.

18th April: "Eagle of Hilbre" (10 tons) owned by Richard Little from Dublin, 2 cases Brockfells, 1 ½ cases Checkers (cloth with a check pattern).

Such was the traffic that a Custom House was established to deal with "great smuggling which went on in the old days when the ships stole quietly up the Dee and hid a cargo of contraband, to be removed when an opportunity occurred." The importance of Hilbre as a port continued to grow in the days of Queen Elizabeth and Cromwell, the Irish wars requiring regular despatches of troops and stores.

It is, perhaps, difficult to imagine the island being put to any kind of industrial or commercial use; but in 1692 a small works was set up to refine rock salt, brought from the great salt mines of Cheshire, into white granulated salt. Likewise there was a beer-house on the island at the height of its days as an anchorage; but when the sea traffic deserted the Dee for the port of Liverpool, the inn shut down for lack of custom. Part of the inn is now incorporated into the Custodian's residence.

The Hilbre Islands were bought by the Trustees of the Liverpool Docks the Mersey Docks and Harbour Board) in 1856, who in turn sold them to Hoylake UDC, in 1945 for £2,500. During local government reorganisation in 1974, Hilbre came into the possession of Wirral Borough Council.

The importance of these small islands to geologists, bird-watchers, nature lovers, or those who simply want to "get away from it all" for a while, has been recognised in their designation as a "Site of Special Scientific Interest" by the Nature Conservancy Council; Wirral Borough Council has also declared the area a Statutory Local Nature Reserve.

Join me, then, on a visit across the Sands of Dee and we shall see if we can capture that special flavour only to be found in this wilderness of sky, sand and sea. But first, a word or two of warning. Near though the island appear from the mainland, do not be tempted to cross straight across the sands towards the main island; deep channels and treacherous mudbanks not visible from the shore make this a dangerous crossing. There is only one safe way; from the slipway at the bottom of Dee Lane at West Kirby, head toward the left-hand side of the Little Eye (the first of the three islands in the group). Once at the Little Eye, keep to the seaward side of the islands until Hilbre itself is reached. The state of the tide must be heeded before crossing. It is usually possible to walk across to Hilbre three hours after high tide; the return trip should be made at least three hours before the next high tide. Visitors wishing to remain on the islands over a high tide should leave the mainland at least three hours before high water. Obviously weather conditions and other variables affect the height and time of the tides, and extreme care must be taken in planning before crossing.

Likewise, the weather in the estuary can change in a matter of minutes; fog and rain can suddenly descend to reduce visibility to yards—a compass is essential if the weather seems as all unstable. Appropriate clothing is important—including Wellington boots to protect feet from glass, shells etc. And don't forget the permit which is necessary if you with to visit the main island.

For our visit, I have chosen a day in mid-October—heavy overnight rain has been blown away across inland Britain by a fresh westerly breeze—the sky is clearing, and a fine day is promised. We are early today—high water is mid morning, and we want to stay on the islands over the high tide; moreover, there will probably be fewer people about at this hour.

From the slipway at West Kirby, the sea is nowhere to be seen; and yet was we tramp across the damp sands, we know that within a couple of hours, the water will be several feet deep were we now tread. This thought makes us quicken our footsteps as we make for the Little Eye. Already, the sights, sounds and cares of land are far behind us; the sun is sending its warm rays down on the estuary; and there is a sense of excitement and anticipation in our hearts. On the far side of the estuary, the green hills of Wales beckon as if to say "Come on over, we are not so far away"; but we know that there are five or six miles of deep channels and mudflats twixt here and the safety of the Welsh coast.

There are few signs of birds hereabouts; the sand has dried out, and there is little to attract them. However, as we reached the higher land around the Little Eye, we can make out the water's edge in the distance and, parallel with it, a narrow black band of birds. And across the sands come the faint sounds of the waves and chatter of thousands of sea birds feeding at the edge of the incoming tide.

Around the Little Eye we change direction as we head for the two main island; yet we are still only halfway to our destination. But this is certainly the most interesting part of the walk. Although it is many hours since the tide receded, this rocky plateau linking the islands is interlaced with channels and rock pools. Here are starfish, sea anemones, crabs, shells and seaweed. Here we may see a lone curlew or oyster-catcher poking about amongst the seaweed for some tasty morsel.

Interesting though this stretch is, we have not the time just now to linger; the tide is making fast and the sea is no respecter of persons. There will be a time a-plenty on the return trek—what's more the tide will have left countless creatures high and dry for our perusal.

We soon reach Middle Hilbre, just three acres of springy turf and bracken. This island presents a virtually sheer cliff-face to the sea on all sides. Having no building of any description, not even a shelter, and with its turf ablaze with thrift in summer, it is, to my mind, the best of the group on which to sit out a high tide. It is small enough to wander around on without that "hemmed in" feeling one gets on the Little

Eye. From the cliff-top we get a fine view of the seal colony hauled out half a mile away on the West Hoyle Bank. Although only a mass of black specks to the naked eye, binoculars reveal large numbers of seals splashing about in the water which is now covering the sand. These are grey seals, and their number here have increased steadily over the past fifty years, from a dozen or so in the 1930s to their present population of over 150. Highest numbers are in the spring and summer, and during high water they will swim quite close in to the islands. Their antics are amusing to watch, for they will dive in one place, to emerge minutes later hundreds of yards away. But best of all is their eerie "song", described by Ellison as reminiscent of "the deep, contented mooing of cows, interrupted by the howling of several dogs".

On the seaward side of Middle Hilbre is a tall, narrow cave knows as the Devil's Hole and said to have been used by smugglers. A walk about the base of these rocky cliffs can be fascinating; the geologist is in his element examining the layers of sandstone and pebbles; and the nature lover examining the cracks and crevices for marine life—sea-slaters, barnacles, molluscs and crabs.

But our goal today is the main island where, while the tide is up, we can explore its twelve acres at our leisure. It is but a few minutes to Hilbre from here, but we must hurry, for already the sea is lapping the seaweed-draped rocks on Hilbre's seaward side. Through the gate, up the slipway, and at last we are on Hilbre Island. Having reached our goal, we felt a unique sense of achievement at having beaten the tide!

On the left of the main path across the island is a small freshwater pond, apparently artificial, its purpose unknown. The uncommon two-flowered narcissus grows here, and hereabouts too may be found the Duke of Argyll's Tea Plant, the dried leaves of which when infused make a drinkable tea. The four wooden buildings on the landward side of Hilbre were originally boathouses, but have been converted into holiday homes. Further north is a stone building erected in 1856 as a buoy store, but now too converted into houses. The next building is the Keeper's residence, originally part of the Seagull beer-house and extended in 1841 when the telegraph station was built.

It is only as we reached the highest point of the island, by the coastguard look-out, that we see that Hilbre really *is* an island—for the tide has now completely encircled us, and there is no turning back! Continuing northward, we pass the reinforced sheer cliff-face of a small bay and, at the most northerly point on the island, the remains of a lifeboat station. From here the rippling waters of the Irish Sea stretch away before us in every direction; a hundred yards offshore a seal shows its head briefly but quickly disappears again. The quietness is broken only by the lapping of the waves against the rocks, the cry of the redshank and, in the far distance, the gentle throb-throb of a small fishing boat going out on the tide.

All the time we have been on Hilbre, flocks of birds have been winging across the estuary, twisting and turning with one accord and landing on every patch of vacant space. Obviously, few birds will settle on or about the islands while there are people about, but if bird-watchers keep out of sight, flocks will settle on the rocky ledges around the islands. In fact, on Lion Rock, to the east of Hilbre, birds have been knows to pack so tightly together that dunlin roosted on the back of sleeping knot! To view the birds from close up, some kind of hide is virtually essential. A permanent observatory has been set up on the island, recording to date some 230 species. Small wonder, then, that Hilbre has been visited by such eminent people such as H.R.H. the Duke of Edinburgh and Eric Hosking, the famous bird photographer. it is not for me to detail the birds to be seen here—others have done a far better job than I could ever do—but suffice to say that the variety of bird life at any time of the year is a constant source of wonder and delight to all who come here.

Our time on Hilbre is nearly up, for the tide is receding and the sand is once again being revealed. But before we go, let us scramble down the slippery rocks below the pond to the Lady's Cave. This dark, dank cave has, not surprisingly, had legendary tales woven about it. Ellison's version is as good as any: On a ledge in this cave one of the Benedictines stationed on the island found a dying maiden cast up by the sea. Before she died the monk learned her story. She was the only daughter of the Custodian of Shotwick Castle and against her father's wish had fallen in love with one of his esquires. As fathers did some six hundred years ago, he ordered her to marry the man of his choice, a Welsh knight. Now you have two versions from which to choose. One states that the angry father packed her off in a boat to wed Llewellyn, the Welsh chieftain; the boat was lost on the passage and the unfortunate maiden was washed ashore and died. The other version is rather different, and this shall be my choice. One day, while off the Point of Ayr, sailing to meet the Welshman, her father told her that the esquire she loved was dead, hoping that she would then agree to his plans. The maiden, stricken by the sudden news, fainted and fell overboard, leaving the father crying out in despair that the story was not true. The tide left her high and dry in the cave but, broken-hearted, she died in the presence of the monk.

And, as we sit here, watching the tide ebb across the sands of Dee, shut out from the sun, we can picture the sad scene in all its detail.

On the homeward trek across the wet sands, we feel a little sad to be leaving this sanctuary in the sea. The turnstones are busily searching the rock-pools for titbits; a lonely curlew wings its way across the estuary, its "cor-lee" echoing across the mudflats; the seals are once more basking in the sun on their sandbank. And as we approach the West Kirby beach, the picnickers and shoppers seem oblivious to the different world we have just left. Back on land, the traffic still roars, life goes on. But we will be back—perhaps on a wet and windy day in December, when the storm clouds gather about the Welsh peaks and hailstones bounce off the sands. or on a crisp morning in January when icicles drape the frost-shrouded rocks around Lady's Cave.

The Dee estuary has many moods, many faces. And yet there has been talk of putting a motorway and a barrage across these wild, lonely expanses of sand, sea and marsh, to speed traffic across to North Wales, and to give the thirsty north-west the water it is said to need. Such schemes would provide facilities for power boating, water-skiing and a dozen other water sports, say the planners. Perhaps, but what about the hundred thousand birds who travel vast distances each year to make this their winter home? Or the colony of seals whose home is the lonely sandbank? Or the glorious mosaic of sunshine and cloud playing across the dappled blue waters? Or those people who just want somewhere where they can be away from the rush, noise and fumes of motor car and lorry, away from the shops, roads and houses, alone with the sand, the sea and the birds—people who, like the Benedictine monks a thousand years ago, just wanted peace and quiet?

THE WIRRAL PENINSULA

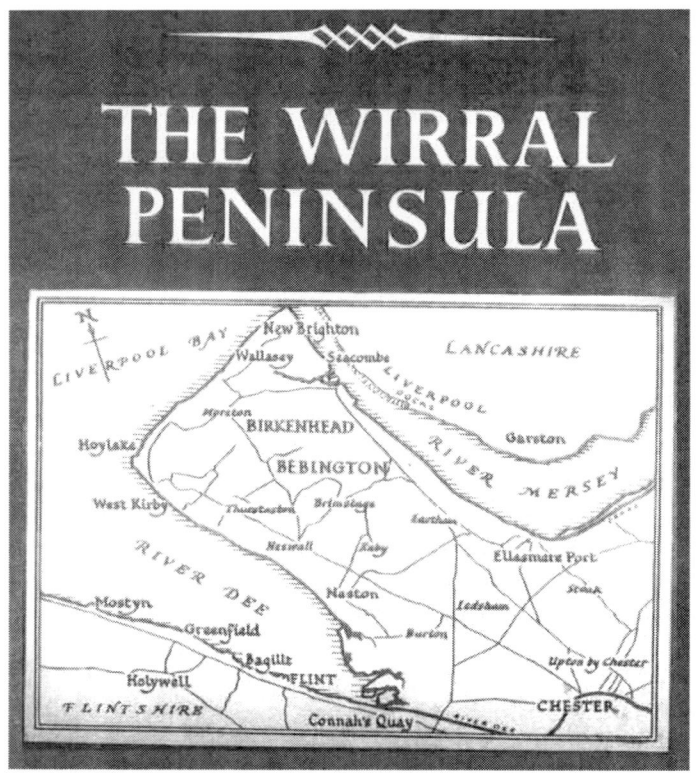

WALLASEY, AND LEASOWE AND SEACOMBE

"Wallasey for wreckers,
Poulton for trees;
Liscard for honest men,
And Seacombe for thieves."

Old Saying

Wirral was a desperate place, the inhabitants were nearly all wreckers and smugglers. They habitually carried on the trade, luring ships onto the banks of the Dee and surrounding areas. There setting about the plunder and pillage of the said vessel, not a care about the death and destruction. A merry time for these waylayers and looters.

Seacombe is where the Barringtons reside. Wallasey, named from ancient times as "Walea" or, Wael As-Eig (Anglo Saxon), Welshman's or Stranger's Island. Such was the prestige of Wallasey, that a new tunnel was built to link it with Merseyside. The new Queensway tunnel was opened on 18th July 1934 and has its entrance on Scotland Road, near Liverpool City Centre. New Brighton to the north of the Wirral was a well established resort in the 50s and 60s, renowned all over Merseyside and the North West of England. Ferries would bulge with holidaymakers in summer, people would flock to its beaches.

Up until the 70s it was a delightful place to visit and explore. Especially for children and the youth of the day. They could take their bucket and spade, their bat and ball. Walk the beaches with their sweethearts, holding hands, kissing, embracing, linking arms in the fine sunlight, strolling along the prom and pier. Leaving the hard living standards of Liverpool and the working class environment that pervaded their world

DEE IMAGES

*A lone curlew flies across a small brook which trickles out of the
wet moorlands high in the Welsh mountains. Gathering life and force,
the brook leaps down hillsides to become a stately river, tumbling over
smooth rocks and flowing gently through quiet green meadows.
At last, it leaves behind its youth and flows, as if beckoned
by some life-force, towards the sea.
Here, with Welsh lands on one bank, and Wirral lands
on the other, it broadens out into a fine and elegant estuary, a vast waste
of marsh, mudflats and sandbanks.*

*The river barely washes Wirral-side with its old Dee ports and villages,
its red cliffs and its sandy beaches. But the Dee still dominates;
from our Wirral lands we see the sun set over its wide, wet reaches; we hear
its waters racing across the mudflats; and we hear a curlew calling
across the sands—the same bird that sped across this rivers at its birth,
high up in those Welsh Hills? Perhaps.*

MERSEY IMAGES

The gulls scream and dance above the foaming wake of the little ferry-boat
as it sails across the grey waters of this great river.
From the top deck of the boat can be seen almost the whole of the
Wirral bank of the Mersey, from New Brighton down past Birkenhead and
beyond Bromborough towards Eastham.
Commerce commands the scene; and that is right,
for this river was tamed for trade, and on trade it developed
and grew to world stature and dominion.
The docks, public buildings and houses which line the riverbank
for over a dozen miles, each have a story to tell; just a small part of the
many images which are part and parcel of the River Mersey.

VILLAGE & COUNTRY IMAGES

The golden sun rises slowly above dew-soaked pastures,
while a gentle breeze rustles the branches into wakefulness as another day
dawns across the Wirral countryside.
A flock of rooks drifts noisily across the cloud-flecked sky towards
fresh feeding grounds on the other side of the peninsula.
In the villages, life stirs; the farm workers take to the fields; and the
commuters head for the towns. Milk floats and delivery vans
break the peace of the quiet lanes which criss-cross this patchwork quilt of
countryside; and, with the approach of each day, the lone fox slinks back
into the safety of the dark copse by the mere.
These are just a few of the images which make up the beauty and interest
of Wirral's countryside.

WALLASEY

Wallasey is a town within the Metropolitan Borough of Wirral, in Merseyside, <u>England</u>, on the mouth of the River Mersey, at the northeastern corner of the <u>Wirral Peninsula</u>. According to the <u>2001 Census</u>, the town had a total resident population of 58,710.

Wallasey Town Hall

History

Toponymy

The name of Wallasey originates from the Germanic word *Walha*, meaning stranger or foreigner, which is also the origin of the name Wales. The suffix "*-ey*" denotes an island or area of dry land. Originally the higher ground now occupied by Wallasey was separated from the rest of Wirral by the creek

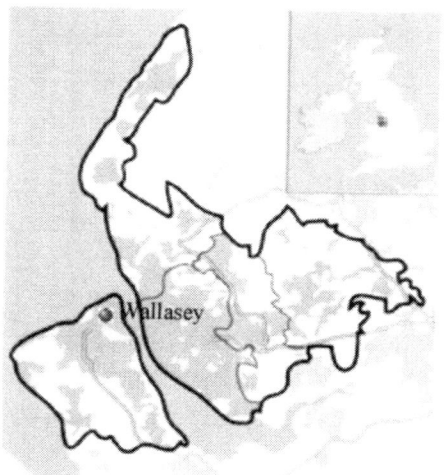

Wallasey shown within Merseyside

known as Wallasey Pool (which later became the docks), the marshy areas of Bidston Moss and Leasowe, and sand dunes along the coast.

Early history

Historically part of Cheshire until 1974, the area was sparsely populated before the 19th century. Horse races organised for the Earls of Derby on the sands at Leasowe in the 16th and 17th centuries are regarded as forerunners of the modern Derby.[2]

Old maps show that the main centre and parish church (St Hilary's) were located at what is now called Wallasey Village, and there were smaller hamlets at Liscard, Poulton and Seacombe, from where there were occasional ferries across the Mersey. There was also a mill (at Mill Lane), and from the mid-18th century a gunpowder store or magazine at Rock Point, located well away from the built-up areas.

The main activities in the area were farming and fishing. The area also had a reputation for smuggling and "wrecking",[3] the act of luring ships onto rocks or sandbanks with false lights in order to raid their cargo. Underground cellars and tunnels, which were used to hide cargo pilfered from wrecked ships still exist in the town.[4] As late as 1839, the "Pennsylvania"

St Hilary's Church

and two other ships were wrecked off Leasowe in a severe storm, and their cargoes and furnishings were later found distributed among local residents.[5]

Early 19th century development

By the early 19th century, the shoreline between Seacombe and Rock Point started to become an attractive area to which affluent Liverpool merchants and sea captains could retire. Development at Egremont began around this time, and gained pace with the introduction of steam ferries across the river. The area also had a defensive role overlooking the growing Port of Liverpool. In 1829, Fort Perch Rock was built, and in 1858 Liscard Battery.

In 1830, the merchant James Atherton purchased much of the land at Rock Point, which enjoyed views out to sea and across the Mersey and had a good beach. His aim was to develop it as a desirable residential and watering place for the gentry, in a similar way to one of the most elegant seaside resorts of that Regency period—hence "New Brighton".

Substantial development began soon afterwards, and housing began to spread up the hillside overlooking the estuary—the gunpowder magazine being closed down in 1851.

In 1835 Liscard Hall was built by another merchant, Sir John Tobin. Its grounds later became Central Park. His family also developed a "model farm" nearby.

With the expansion of trade on the Mersey, new docks were constructed between 1842 and 1847 in the Wallasey Pool, and by 1877 the dock system between Wallasey and neighbouring Birkenhead was largely complete. The area around the docks became a centre for engineering industries, many associated with shipbuilding, and other activities

East Float Dock

including sugar refining and the manufacture of cement and fertilisers. Bidston Dock, the last in the area, was opened in 1933, but was filled in during 2003.[6]

Later growth and the 20th century

During the latter half of the 19th century New Brighton developed as a very popular seaside resort serving Liverpool and the Lancashire industrial towns, and many of the large houses were converted to inexpensive hotels. A pier was opened in the 1860s, and the promenade from Seacombe to New Brighton was built in the 1890s. This served both as a recreational amenity in its own right, and to link up the developments along the estuary, and was later extended westwards towards Leasowe. The New Brighton Tower, the tallest in the country, was opened in 1900 but closed in 1919 and dismantled shortly afterwards. However, its ballroom continued as a major venue, hosting numerous concerts in the 1950s and 1960s by local Liverpool bands as well as other international stars.

After 1886, with the opening of the Mersey Railway allowing access via a tunnel to Liverpool, the pace of housing development increased, particularly in the Liscard and Wallasey Village areas. The area now called Wallasey comprises several distinct districts which gradually merged together to form a single built-up area during the 19th and early 20th centuries. Further growth continued well into the 20th century and eventually spread into the Leasowe area and beyond to Moreton.

The UK's first guide dog training school, the Guide Dogs for the Blind Association, was founded in the town in 1931. The Wallasey Golf Club is where club member, Dr Frank Stableford, developed the Stableford system of points scoring. This was first used in competition in 1932.

Because of its docks and proximity to Liverpool, parts of the area suffered aerial bombing in 1940-41. After the Second World War, the popularity of New Brighton as a seaside resort declined dramatically, as did the use of the docks, and Wallasey gradually became more obviously a residential suburb for Liverpool, Birkenhead and the other towns in the area.

The Beatles played some of their first shows outside Liverpool at the Grosvenor Ballroom in Liscard in 1960, and over the next few years also played several times at the Tower Ballroom in New Brighton. On 12 October 1962, they played there as the support act for Little Richard. Wallasey was also the home base of another leading Merseybeat group, the Undertakers featuring Jackie Lomax.

The world's first passenger hovercraft service operated in 1961-62 between Leasowe and Rhyl in North Wales. Local MP Ernest Marples was responsible as Minister of Transport (1959-64) for introducing parking meters, yellow lines and seat belt controls to the UK.

The "Solar Campus" on Leasowe Road was the first building in the world to be heated entirely by solar energy. It was formerly St George's Secondary School, and was built in 1961 to the designs of Emslie Morgan. The solar panels on this establishment have since been removed due to high costs and has been renamed.

Civic history

Wallasey became a County Borough in 1913, and its town hall opened in 1916. The borough boundaries expanded to include Moreton and Saughall Massie in 1928.

The County Borough of Wallasey was incorporated into the Metropolitan Borough of Wirral on 1 April 1974. The town is contained in the parliamentary constituency of Wallasey, which has been held since the 1992 general election by Angela Eagle of the Labour Party.

Education

When compared to the national average, the schools of Wallasey slightly underperform on GCSE results. However they are above the national average on A Level results.

Primary schools

- Liscard Primary School
- St George's Primary School
- Somerville Primary School
- Riverside Primary School
- Egremont Primary School
- Mount Primary School
- Park Primary School
- New Brighton Primary School
- Greenleas Primary School
- Kingsway Primary School
- St Josephs Primary School
- St Albans Primary School

Secondary schools

- The Mosslands School
- Weatherhead High School
- The Oldershaw School
- Wallasey School
- St Mary's Catholic College

Voluntary aided schools

- St Alban's Catholic Primary School
- St Joseph's Catholic Primary School
- Saints Peter and Paul Catholic Primary School
- St Mary's Catholic College

Geography

The area now called Wallasey comprises several distinct districts—Egremont, Liscard, New Brighton, Poulton, Seacombe and Wallasey Village. These gradually merged together to form a single built-up area during the 19th and early 20th centuries.

Unlike in most other towns, there is no single Wallasey town centre, although the main shopping area is centrally located at Liscard. Both the parliamentary constituency and the former County Borough of Wallasey also include (or included) Leasowe, Moreton and Saughall Massie, which are now usually regarded as separate settlements.

Liscard

This contains the main shopping area, with the covered Cherry Tree precinct and an extensive shopping parade outside. Central Park, originally the grounds of Liscard Hall, is the largest park in the town. Much of the area is residential and contains mainly high-density semi-detached housing with some terraces. The gatehouse of the old Liscard Battery remains.

Liscard Hall was destroyed by a fire on 7 July 2008. The damage was so severe, the whole building had to be demolished.

Wallasey Village

Wallasey Village has a mixture of popular mostly 20th century semi-detached and detached housing, a shopping street, with a floral roundabout in the centre. It is considered the most wealthy area of Wallasey. St Hilary's Church is an ancient foundation; the old tower is all that remains of a 1530 church building which burned down in 1857.

There are two railway stations, Wallasey Village and Wallasey Grove Road. At the north end of Wallasey Village, the main street leads to the promenade and coastal park, and two golf courses. The promenade passes here, running from the 'Gunsite' around to Seacombe, a total of over 7 miles.

New Brighton

New Brighton was a popular seaside resort after the mid-19th century, but declined in popularity after the 1950s. Nevertheless, the marine promenade is part of a popular walk and the areas near the sea offer a much improved beach and many leisure activities. The Floral Pavilion plays host to regular productions and national stars

New Brighton Lighthouse on Perch Rock.

such as Ken Dodd, and Vale Park is a beautiful public park. Housing here ranges from large villas near the sea to suburban semi-detached homes, while there are some less attractive terraces in parts of the area. New Brighton is served by a railway station of the same name. New Brighton promenade is the UK's longest promenade.

Poulton

Poulton was originally a small fishing and farming hamlet beside the Wallasey Pool (hence its name). It developed with the growth of the docks, mainly as an industrial and terraced housing area.

Egremont

Egremont developed as an affluent residential area in the early 19th century, and was named by one Captain Askew who built a house in the area in 1835 and named it after his Cumberland birthplace. Egremont Pier was built in 1827 and was the longest pier on Merseyside until it was damaged irreparably in 1946 when a coaster collided with it. Wallasey Town Hall, an imposing edifice opened in 1916 and initially used as a war hospital, is located here, overlooking the estuary and with its back to the town. This area is now almost entirely housing, although there is a small shopping area on King Street.

Seacombe

Seacombe, the most southeasterly section of Wallasey, is best known for its Mersey Ferry terminal, with regular ferry boat departures to Pier Head in Liverpool and Woodside in Birkenhead. There is a commuter ferry service direct to Liverpool during peak hours, while for the rest of the day the ferries are geared to serving tourists with a circular cruise visiting Birkenhead Woodside ferry terminal as well. Seacombe is the last remaining of the three ferry terminals which used to connect the Borough of Wallasey, the others being Egremont Ferry and the New Brighton Ferry, which operated from its own pier, running parallel to the New Brighton pleasure pier. Seacombe Ferry is also the starting point of a four mile unbroken promenade, mostly traffic-free, running alongside the River Mersey to Harrison Drive beyond New Brighton.

Local landmarks are St Paul's Church, standing on its own traffic island, and the ventilation tower for the Kingsway Tunnel with its mighty extraction fans. As with Poulton, the area developed with housing for the dockworkers and nearby industries, and much of the housing is owned by Wirral Partnership Homes or are terraced. The Guinea Gap swimming baths are located between Seacombe and Egremont.

Transport

Road

- The Kingsway Tunnel, Opened by Queen Elizabeth II when it was completed in 1971, its roadway route via Poulton leads to its entrance in Seacombe, which links Wallasey with the centre of Liverpool and is set to be featured in Harry Potter and the Deathly Hallows Part 1
- The M53 motorway begins in Poulton and leads south through the centre of the Wirral Peninsula to Chester and the M56 motorway continues to Manchester Airport.
- The North Wallasey Approach Road begins in Wallasey Village and ends in Bidston at Junction 1 of the M53.
- Leasowe Road gives access to Leasowe and Moreton to the west, and to Wallasey Village to the east.

Rail

Present

There are three railway stations: Wallasey Village, Wallasey Grove Road and New Brighton. Electric trains to Liverpool and Birkenhead depart every 15 minutes (every 30 minutes during late evenings and on Sundays). Grove Road station has a large car park with over 160 spaces. There are also railway stations located in Leasowe and Moreton on the railway to West Kirby.

Past

Formerly, an additional railway line ran from Seacombe (& Egremont) station to Wrexham. An intermediate station served Liscard & Poulton. The line, and both stations, closed to passengers in 1960 when the trains were diverted to New Brighton. Subsequently these trains were diverted away from Wallasey to start from Birkenhead North and nowadays from Bidston. The cutting where the line once ran now forms the approach road to the Kingsway Tunnel, and Seacombe station site was developed for housing.

Bus

Regular bus services (Arriva routes 432 and 433) depart Liscard every 10 minutes and travel via the Kingsway Tunnel to Liverpool. In addition, there are several services which link the districts of Wallasey and nearby towns such as Birkenhead, Leasowe and Moreton.

Until 1969, Wallasey had its own corporation bus service; from this date the operation was taken over by Merseyside Passenger Transport Executive. The Wallasey bus service was relatively constrained within the borough boundaries, and had two distinctive features. One was the unusual livery, which appeared to be two shades of yellow (officially it was "sea green" and rich cream, but it always looked yellow and the service was generally known as the "yellow buses"). Secondly the services mostly radiated from Seacombe Ferry terminal across the borough, and bus departures coincided with the arrival of the ferry. Vehicles were lined up facing outwards from the kerb and every 10-15 minutes the passengers (several hundreds at peak hours) would arrive from the ferry boat. When all had boarded their respective routes the inspector in charge would blow a whistle and there would be an amazing Le Mans-style start with up to fifteen double-decker buses, including racing engines, close manoeuvring, and competitive gestures between the crews, for the first few hundred yards until the routes gradually diverged across the borough.

Notable people

The following people were born in Wallasey:

- Samuel John "Lamorna" Birch (1869-1955), painter
- Olaf Stapledon (1886-1950), science fiction writer and philosopher
- Walter McLennan Citrine, Baron Citrine, GBE, PC (1887-1983), trade unionist and politician
- Saunders Lewis (1893-1985), Welsh nationalist politician and writer
- Major Bill Tilman, CBE, DSO, MC and Bar (1898-1977), mountaineer and explorer
- Sidonie Goossens (1899-2004), harpist
- Frank Doel (1908-1968), bookseller in London, whose story is told in *84 Charing Cross Road*
- Malcolm Lowry (1909-1957), writer (*Under the Volcano*)
- Charles Crichton (1910-1999), film director (*The Lavender Hill Mob, A Fish Called Wanda*)
- Leslie Graham (1911-1953), world champion motorcycle racer
- Deryck Guyler (1914-1999), actor and comedian
- Raymond Moore, (1920-1987), photographer
- Graham Stark (b 1922), actor
- General Sir Miles Dempsey GBE,KCB,DSO,MC (1896-1969) commander of the British Second Army during the D-Day landings
- Dickie Davies (b 1933), TV sports journalist and presenter
- Rita Hunter CBE (1933-2001), opera singer
- Ralph Steadman (b 1936), artist and cartoonist
- Ann Bell (b 1940), actress
- Geoffrey Hughes (b 1944), actor
- Michael Carson (b 1946), writer
- Nigel Olsson (b 1949), rock drummer (Elton John)
- Alan Rouse (1951-1986), mountaineer
- Ray Stubbs (b 1956), TV sports presenter
- Louise Delamere (b 1969), actress
- Dominic Purcell, (b 1970), actor
- Elizabeth Berrington, (b 1970), actress
- Austin Healey (b 1973), Leicester and England Rugby Union player
- Jenny Frost, (b 1978), singer (member of Atomic Kitten)
- Jay Spearing (b 1988), Liverpool F.C. defender and defensive midfielder

Eric Idle, of *Monty Python* fame, lived in Wallasey between the ages of three and nine (1946-1952). Other former residents include Matthew Smith, games programmer who developed several well-known titles for the Sinclair ZX Spectrum in the 1980s; and Simon "Sice" Rowbottom (b 1969) and Timothy Brown from the band the Boo Radleys. England International darts player Robbie "Kong" Green lives in the town.

The St Clair's of Rosslyn were one of the most prestigious families in Scotland. They rubbed shoulders with kings and the royalty of those lands. They engaged in wars against the English and stood in battle with the likes of William Wallace and Robert the Bruce.

The Rosslyn name came about when the village of Roslin once held a castle. This sanctified part of the world was considered sacred, a chapel was built in honour of the knights Templar and the veneration of the Holy Grail. Other mysteries, hidden secrets and the manifestation of the Masonic Society. The Masons of past history who built the temples for the enlightenment of the world. For those who endeavour to follow the path of righteousness and faith of Templar belief. For the pilgrims of the faithful journey from the shrine of St James of Compostela to Rosslyn. This is a narrative, a story in detail of the quest by the initiated to be spiritually fulfilled.

ROSSLYN CHAPEL AND SPIRITUAL FULFILMENT

osslyn Chapel is the natural starting point in any rational search for clues to the methods of initiation used in the late medieval era. Created as a superbly carved reliquary for the Grail, which in itself is nothing less than an allegorical description of the path to enlightenment, it is also the ultimate pinnacle of the pilgrimage of initiation which was sacred to the memory and beliefs of the Knights Templar, and tradition tell us us that their heirs used a hidden room under the chapel as in initiation chamber. The paucity of archival records of Templar beliefs makes the task of interpreting their romantic legends realistically extremely difficult.

It has been long recognised that the chapel was a site of special veneration and pilgrimage. Folklore recounts how pilgrims in their thousands travelled there after completing the arduous trek to the shrine of St James of Compostela. I had suggested in an earlier work that this may have been because of some relic kept at Rosslyn, a Black Madonna perhaps, though other authors do not agree with me; in *the Hiram Key* this possibility was dismissed. The association of the Templars with the Black Madonna, however, is a matter of recorded fact. Ean Begg's book, *the Cult of the Black Madonna*, is perhaps the best-known exposition of this strange cult.

In describing their research into ancient Israel *The Hiram Key* the authors did not mention the esoteric significance of the name of Israel itself. It is held to stand for Isis RA and Elohim, thus recording the three divine Egyptian and Canaanite roots of Hebraic gnosticism; the very foundation for the hidden streams which pervade and illuminate Judaeo-Christian spirituality. But why did such knowledge have to remain hidden?

The medieval Christian Church was the most intolerant and repressive authority that Europe has ever experienced. After the suppression of the Templar Order, their spiritual heirs had once again to disguise their initiatory processes under the cloak of acceptable Christian ritual and practice. What better than for it novices to make a series of ostensibly devout Christian pilgrimages to the cathedrals built on the seven sacred sites of the prophetic configuration?

Trevor Ravenscroft had often suggested that even before the advent of Christianity, Celtic pilgrims who worshipped the Earth goddess journeyed from Iberia to Scotland via the seven planetary oracles, associating the alignment of the spirit senses within themselves to the corresponding alignment of the Earth chakras. The sequence of the sites corresponds to that of the planets in our solar system; the Moon, Mercury, Venus, the Sun, Mars, Jupiter and Saturn. There was no arbitrary choice involved in which seven cathedrals were an integral part of this apocalyptic configuration in stone.

Bounded by the pillars at either end, the seven sacred sites lie under the beneficent royal arch of the Milky Way. Trevor was convinced that this powerful configuration is not static; he believed that must as subliminal energies stream up and down through the chakras within the human body, so similar forces, the Wouivre, surge northwards and southwards along this great alignment of cathedrals. Dowsers have discovered that powerful lines of energy intersect at each of the sites along this route.

There was a complex web of inter-connecting routes to Compostela from all over Europe. The pilgrimage began to gain immense popularity during the reign of Charlemagne (768-814 AD), but the main guide for the intending pilgrims was published in the twelfth century as the Codex Callextinus. Included on the various itineraries were Amiens, St Denis in Montmartre, Notre-Dame de Paris, Chartres, Orleans, Tours, Poitiers, Le Puy and Toulouse.

Most of the seven sites of the configuration were on different routes to Compostela. Trevor Ravenscroft was convinced that insightful pilgrims journeyed from Compostela to Rosslyn, calling at each of the sites in turn. I have learnt since his death that his perceptions have almost invariably proved to be uncannily accurate. So, could he have been right in some mysterious way, and if he was what did it signify?

One of the keys to this puzzle proved to lie in applying an understanding of the Druidic concept that the seven sacred sites were the earthly equivalent of the seven chakras or energy centres in human beings. This idea that there are seven Earth power points arcing across Western Europe from northern Spain to Scotland has been confirmed from other sources. What relevance has that to Rosslyn Chapel, other than the fact the Rosslyn is the seventh site in the alignment?

The Path to Enlightenment

Attaining enlightenment in the Western esoteric tradition involved a form of ritualised mysticism wherein the novice was taught and guided by a Master. These seven chakras were ritually awakened in a predetermined order, from the base upward to the crown. When the powers of spirit and matter combined, the seven chakras acted as a single channel. This energetic power followed a winding path as it moved between the centres. In Eastern schools of philosophy it is described as the raising of the serpent known as the Kundalini, which then moves through the other chakras as the student ascends to the higher levels of awareness. It is not surprising that the esoteric symbol associated with the Wouivre, the telluric force recognised by the Druids and the Templars, is the serpent. The specific order of the awakening of energy centres from the base to the crown explains why, in the pilgrimage of initiation, the ritual order of progress is a complete reversal of the normal, orthodox pilgrimage to Compostela.

As each chakra is energetically opened the student, spiritually speaking, makes progress. Thus the pilgrimage is not simply one journey encompassing each of the seven sites, but a series of journeys made in a predetermined order, starting with the Druid Moon Oracle at Compostela, representing the base chakra, then moving northwards to each site in the alignment in turn before culminating at Rosslyn, representing the crown chakra. Each stage is only accomplished after an appropriate period of intense and spiritual preparation.

The novice making an initiatory pilgrimage to the shrine of St James by one of the routes laid down in the Codex Callextinus had demonstrated sufficient dedication and humility to qualify for the sublime gift of illumination. The achievement of this stage revealed a twofold quality of humility and obedience. The first was outwardly to the diktat of Holy Mother the Church; the second, and hidden form, was to his teacher and, through him, to his ultimate master, Almighty God.

First-degree initiation was the result the flowed spiritually from the awakening of the base chakra that connects us with the earth and physical reality; according to tradition it can only be opened after the attainment of true humility, for this is the chakra that literally keeps us rooted. In the human body it controls the base of the spine, and is closely link with the adrenals, and therefore represents that most basic of all instincts, survival. The first degree, the Raven, symbolised the messenger of the gods. it was thus that the new candidate achieved, through inner toil, the first stage of soul conversion through which he gained the capacity to received messages from spirits in the divine world. The Raven also represented the messenger of the mystery cults who had learned to express the visual images which could be understood at different levels by both the outside world and by the initiated.

When the novice had progressed thus far along his chosen spiritual path, he was open to receive the messenger of the mystery cults. He would then be instructed to make the pilgrimage from Compostela to Toulouse, to the church built on the site of the Mercury oracle. Mercury was simple the Latinisation of the Greek god Hermes, the winged messenger of the gods. At Toulouse he would be introduced to the mysteries of the second degree with the opening of the sacral or abdominal chakra, which lies between the base and solar plexus centres and works closely with them. The second degree is known as that of the Occultist and is symbolised by the Peacock, whose many-splendoured plumage represents the student's new powers of moral imagination. This was known to have been gained when he discovered his own inner space and could retire into the hidden isolation of his own spirit. He had become the Hidden One, or Occultist, who could now communicate directly with Hermes Trismegistus, the thrice-blessed one of the Green mysteries whose bust adorns the eastern wall of Rosslyn Chapel.

The Knight was the symbol of the third and warrior degree and knighthood was bestowed for the attainment of it. When the aspirant had gained sufficient inner strength and moral courage to represent the good against the evil in the world, he was named the Warrior. The legendary Knights of the Round Table of King Arthur were initiates at this level, as were the Knights Templar who were able to represent the sword of justice in the barbaric medieval world. The fulfilment of this degree led to the awakening of the third chakra, said to be the storehouse of prana, the universal life-force. When fear and anxiety register here, thought becomes action. Many people see another linkage with the adrenals because of the fight-or-flight syndrome brought about by the action of adrenaline. This degree was achieved by entry into the mysteries of the Venus oracle at the sublime Cathedral of Orleans.

When suitably qualified candidates were prepared for further advancement along their chosen spiritual path they would visit the site of the heart chakra and undergo the initiation in the mystical underground chamber of la Vierge de Sous-Terre in the crypt of Chartres Cathedral, the ancient site of the Sun oracle. There they were accorded the degree of the Lion. The Swan was the sacred symbol of this, the fourth degree, because the swansong represented the death of self and the inner realization of the divine within the human breast. The fourth degree was only awarded when the aspirant had gained control of his subjective processes so that no unconscious prejudice could rule his actions. At this level of spiritual development the divine element within him had become so strong that he could look into the core of his own being and shrink from no toil which duty demanded of him.

This degree was mirrored by the awakening of the heart chakra, often called the Abode of Mercy, which is linked to the region of the thymus gland above the heart. This centre represents the union between the physical and spiritual aspects of the personality. It controls the individual's emotions and how they related to others and to nature. Most importantly it is the spiritual centre controlling the sublime gifts of love and compassion. The colour traditionally attributed to this chakra is green, the colour of initiation and birth.

The first four degrees, the Raven, the Occultist, the Warrior, and the Lion, all represent the spiritual transformation of toil; the fifth and sixth degrees were gained through the spiritualisation of suffering. Induction into the fifth degree was performed in the chamber under Notre-Dame de Paris, the site of the Druidic oracle of Mars, and in Grail symbolism was depicted by the Pelican, the bird which wounds its own breast to feed its young. Such an initiate lived for the perpetuation of his own people, being granted their name—for instance, the Persian, the Egyptian, the Greek, or the Israelite—and dedicated his life to their service. He now worked within a conscious unity of the folk-spirit of his people, that is, he could suffer the responsibility of speaking for his own karmic community. The fifth centre is the throat chakra, and is the first of the higher ones. It is associated with communication and demands that a distinction be made between purposeful words and thought, and those which are idle and meaningless noise. it is the centre of both speech and inner hearing, and is connected with the power of sound.

The brow chakra, known to many as the third eye, or eye of the mind, is connected with the centre, which relates to the right side of the brain to the spiritual faculties of insight and intuition; it brings a direct 'knowing'. It is responsible for the balance and harmony of the energy system. When his chakra was awakened the, by know, highly qualified aspirant would be instructed in the sublime mysteries of the Jupiter oracle and gain advancement to the sixth and penultimate degree, denoted by the Eagle. This took place in the glorious confines of the Cathedral of Amiens, where he acquired the capacity to move and communicate in the spiritual world and gained a true insight into the secrets of space; he could expand his consciousness between Earth and Sun within the streaming of time.

All who were privileged enough to undertake this pilgrimage would have been spiritually gifted men, and those who rose to attain any of the higher degrees of initiation would have been men of exceptional talent, humility and dedication. There were only twenty four men of supreme talent in the influential early Renaissance Order of the Golden Fleece, of which Earl William St Clair was a member. Was this chivalric Order the outward face of the Rex Deus families who claimed descent from the twenty four High Priests of the Jerusalem Temple? Or was this perhaps the overt face of that secretive, select few who had finally achieved the highest order of them all: the Kings of the Grail?

The Crown was the royal symbol of the King of the Grail. To him was revealed an understanding of all the laws at work within human destiny. The holder of the seventh degree was given the name of 'the Father' because the initiate knew the secrets of time and had gained a true understanding of the working of the primal karma out of which the father-God was functioning.

This degree gave an insight into the spiritualisation of death, which may have explained the ancient Knights Templar's well-deserved reputation for being fearless in battle. It was attained with the culmination of the spiritual journey at the opening of the crown chakra, which is mystically united with the pineal gland; known to the devotees of the Greek mysteries as the Seat of the Soul—the seat of consciousness and the doorway to the creator. Even the supreme rationalist Descartes claimed that the pineal linked body and soul. This chakra is sometime regarded as a unique centre of consciousness and therefore separate from the other six. Its opening is essential for attaining complete attunement in the processes of both healing and meditation. The full flowering of the crown chakra occurs when the head of the serpent-like kundalini reaches it, for which the psychological keyword is Awakening.

The enlightenment which flows from the opening of the crown chakra is the supreme and total fulfilment of the Grail search, and was awarded at the seventh site, Rosslyn Chapel, the ancient and revered site of the Saturn oracle itself. The initiation ceremony for this degree took place in the hidden chamber under the chapel which was deliberately created by Earl William St Clair as the focal point for every known path of initiation. Rosslyn Chapel—the Omphalos or spiritual umbilicus of the world.

Omphalos (in the ancient world) a sacred conical object, especially a stone. The famous omphalos at Delphi was assumed to mark the centre of the earth; the centre point; literally; another word for navel.

Other Pilgrims

There is evidence confirming this concept of the pilgrimage of initiation in scriptural sources and elsewhere. Biblical mention of the ravens who fed Elijah are held to mark the beginning of his path of initiation. The events at Serepha where he heals the son of the widow show him to be a Hidden One who has achieved the second degree. On Mount Carmel he defends the knowledge of the spirit, and as a Warrior represents the good in the fight against evil. On Horeb, when he perceives Jehovah within his own soul, he achieves the fourth degree, that of the Lion. His later achievement of the final three degrees were revealed to Elisha, who inherited his mantle on the occasion of Elijah's assumption into heaven, when his pupil saw the fiery chariot of the sun hero drawn by horses across the heavens. Elisha describes the vision in these words 'My Father, my Father, the chariot of Israel and the horses thereof.' In a single magnificent flight of imagination, Elisha describes the genius of Israel, the spirit of the sun-hero and the sphere of the Father.

Glen and Rosa were intrigued by the romance and mysticism surrounding Rosslyn Chapel, the Knights Templar and the Pilgrimage of the Seven Chakras. In fact, Glen and Rosa were married at the Rosslyn Chapel at the time of the summer solstice around the time of June 21st when the sun is at its northern-most point in the heavens, taking their vows on the Sunday 20th June 1976. And a glorious day it was. The bride had rosebuds in her flaxen hair, and a gold tiara rested atop her chignon-styled locks. A light chiffon veil covered her sparkling pearl grey eyes, and fell like a waterfall over her shoulders and down her back to the hips. The soft white satin halter neck dress blazed bright, gleaming in the midday sun. An amber necklace hung low upon the delicately exposed cleavage. A white three inch leather belt with a decorative gold laurel leaf buckle hugged her corsage. Pleats split the evenness of the dress, ending one inch below the knee. Her bronzed toned bare legs complemented the white stiletto heeled shoes emblazoned with a red rose on their uppers. It was sheer delight, she looked like an angel. Glen holding on to Rosa hand over his left arm, their faces beaming with happiness as they emerged from the porch. Tourists gathered, bag pipes played and guard of honour stood in sovereign salute.

The groom looked magnificent in his captains uniform. His army footwear was polished beyond infinity. Black close fitting trousers with thin red stripes down the sides rose to a breast coat of vibrant red. A gold and crimson sash encircled the waist. A rapier-like sword dangled from its sling. Gleaming silver buttons were fastened up to a high necked decorative collar. Studded epaulettes adorned the shoulders. Embroidered cuffs and pristine white gloves complemented the military attire. Glen was statuesque, Rosa was stunning. The colours blended stupendously as they both walked almost marching under the ceremonial guard of honour that his comrades had prepared. A fairy tale wedding, a majestic occasion seen by the lucky few in the bathing sunlight of Rosslyn Chapel.

The Scots Guards are a regiment of the British Army. The regiment cherishes its traditions, especially on the parade ground where the scarlet uniform and bearskin have become synonymous with the regiment and the other Guards regiments. The regiment takes part in numerous events, most notably Beating the Retreat, Changing of the Guard,

Queen's Birthday Parade, Remembrance Sunday and State Visits. The Guard's regiments ceremonial uniforms differ from each other only slightly, the differentiations being in the tunic and the type of plume on the bearskin, if any, they have. The Scots Guards uniform consists of tunic buttons in threes, the Order of the Thistle on the shoulder badge, the Thistle on the collar badge and no plume on the bearskin.

On 2nd April 1982, Argentina, then under a dictatorship led by General Galtieri, invaded the British territory of the Falklands Islands off South America. The British soon assembled a large array of Royal Navy (RN) warships, Royal Fleet Auxiliaries and merchant ships and headed south for Ascension Island. On the 25 April, the island of South Georgia, off Antarctica was recaptured and on the 1 May the RN Carrier Battle Group had entered the 200-mile (370 km) Total Exclusion Zone (TEZ) which had been placed around the Falklands. On 12 May the 2nd Battalion, as part of the 5th Infantry Brigade (1st Battalion, The Welsh Guards, 1st/7th Duke of Edinburgh's Own Gurkha Rifles), embarked aboard RMS Queen Elizabeth 2 (QE2), which had been requisitioned by the Government for use as a troopship, and departed Southampton for South Georgia. In the early hours of the 21 May D-Day began with 3 Commando Brigade (including two Para battalions) landing unopposed at San Carlos water and successfully established a bridgehead.

In late May the QE2 arrived at her destination but because she could not be risked by moving her closer to the Falklands, most of the 5th Brigade were transferred to the P & O liner SS Canberra who would then take them to their destination. On the 2nd June, Canberra anchored in San Carlos Water, and subsequently the Guards were landed at San Carlos by LCU, a day after the 1st/7th Gurkhas had been landed by LCU from the ferry Norland. On 5th June the Scots Guards were embarked aboard the assault ship HMS Intrepid before being transferred to the ship's four LCUs who transported them to Bluff Cove. On 8th June the 1st Welsh Guards were aboard RFA Sir Galahad also waiting to be landed at Bluff Cove when Sir Galahad and RFA Sir Tristram were attacked by Argentinian Skyhawk fighters who proceeded to hit both ships. Sir Galahad was terribly hit and both ships caught fire, causing terrible casualties aboard Sir Galahad. Forty eight people, including thirty two Welsh Guards, were killed and many were wounded, many suffering from terrible burns. Unfortunately, only 200 survived.

On the morning of 13 June the Scots Guards were moved from their positions at Bluff Cove by helicopter to an assembly area near Goat Ridge near to their objective, Mount Tumbledown, which was defended by a crack Argentinan unit, the 5th Marine Infantry Battalion. On the night of the 13th the main force of the Scots Guards began its advance on the western side of Mount Tumbledown. During the course of the battle in the early hours of the 14th, men of the battalion launched a bayonet charge on the stout Argentinia defenders which resulted in bitter and bloody fighting, and was one of the last bayonet charges by the British Army. The battled raged on and by 8.00 am the final objective was taken and Mount Tumbledown was in the hands of the Scots Guards. The battle had been bloody, yet successful, and the battalion had proven the elite calibre and professionalism of the regiment in taking a well-defended mountain, defended by a top Argentinian unit, for it had been performing public duties back in London only a few months before. The Scots Guards casualties were eight Guards and one Royal Engineer killed and forty three wounded. Their Argentinian opponents lost forty men and over thirty captured.

On 14 June the Argentinian commander surrendered his forces of just under 10,000 men to the British, the war was over, though the end of hostilities would not officially be declared until the 20 June. The following day, Juiliet Company (made up mostly of men of Naval Party 8901 who had defended the Falklands when it had been invaded) raised the Governor's flag above Government House, it had been down for seventy four days; the Falklands were finally liberated. Most of 5th Brigade were moved back to Fitzroy and the Scots Guards were subsequently moved to West Falkland to await the arrival of the first garrison troops and eventually departed the Falklands for Ascension on Norland on 19 July. The battalion was subsequently returned home by air, being transported by RAF VC-10 aircraft. The regiment won a number of gallantry awards for their actions in the Falklands War. A single Distinguished Service Order (DSO) was won, being awarded to the battalion's CO Lieutenant-Colonel Michael Scott. Also won by the battalion were two Military Crosses (MC), two Distinguished Conduct Medals (DCM) and two Military Medals (MM). The battalion was awarded two battle honours for its part in the war. "Tumbledown Mountain" and "Falkland Islands 1982".

Glen was in this war. Rosa was still active with her promotional work and modeling, mostly hand and voice overs for adverts. She was thirty so still she was eligible for photo shoots on the beach and holiday brochures. But her dressmaking was taking off in a big way in the eighties. Tony was a child of two in this year so most of her time was done caring for her first born. But there was a nanny and Gerta had arrived on the scene and became an integral part of the family. It would be a worrying time with Glen away on duty in the cold Antarctica environment.

After his short tour of Belfast in Ireland, Rosa was used to the army element in her life but she felt her husband would be protected and return safe and sound. Not sadly for some of the heroic soldiers who stood along side him in conflict. Her heart was waiting for it to be all over. That time would be in the year 2000 when Glen retired. His one abiding memory was receiving his Distinguished Conduct Medal (DCM) after the battle of Bluff Cove. But at this moment in time fate and fortune was uppermost, life giving and monumentally awe inspiring.

SPRING 1969

Rosa was noticed by an executive of a modeling company dealing in clothes and make up, the day Rosa was helping at a gypsy fair in Bournemouth, a massive bring and buy arts and crafts fair held only once a year by the Council. She was a spring flower, a budding rose. Mum was there, they had already made five hundred pounds on their home made clothes, jewelry, assorted curios of objet d'art, ornaments and trinkets.

The sun was glorious, it was 1969. There was a mystic element in the air. "Here's my card!" passing it over between his forefinger and thumb in a direct confident way. Rosa's eyes almost transparent and alive with a magnificent shine, glanced up shyly and fluttered her long eyelashes innocently and softly. "Come and work for me, I will make you a star and a lot of money of course!". The Managing Director Keith Reader smiled with empathy. Rosa's mother took the card and in her delightful broken but elegant speech she agreed to talk it over with her daughter at a more convenient time.

Her daughter would finish school later that year and she knew in her heart this would be the path that her only off spring would be taking. A moment of inspiration that could influence her life and fortune. Rosa was seventeen, it would be time for a new era, a calling, a vocation. The hard but lucrative gypsy lifestyle was not forecast for the talented and sensational Rosa. Gypsies have been given a somewhat down case reputation over the decades. Romany or Romanian, another name for gypsies belonging to the Indian branch of indo-European families have been labeled as lowly musicians. The Davidian tribes pushed south from India. Wandering nations of people developing their own brands of uniqueness flooding England and Europe. Gradually centuries have seen these traveling folk educate and prosper to great heights.

There is a wide spectrum of gypsy employments from the sale of goods not made by the travelers, the offer of services, seasonal labour, and the provision of goods and services produced largely by the gypsies. It was not always clear in which category a particular employment should be placed. For example, fairground entertaining could be described as both a seasonal employment and a service; the gypsies made some of the pegs and baskets while others were bought from a wholesaler; and the link between hawking items and fortune telling was such that the offer of goods and a particular service went hand in hand at times.

A further separation of labor can be made by adding the division between the various types of employment according to gender. The men were at various times in occupations that could be under any of the aforementioned categories, but it was common for women to be employed only in the service or craft trades. In general, the men manufactured craft items while it was the responsibility of the women to take on the role of selling, or hawking, items of services door to door.

The music of the gypsy was well known and followed by many gypsies and non-gypsies. The chief characteristic of the music played by the gypsies bore the freedom, richness, variety and versatility of its rhythms. These characteristics constantly changed, intertwined, intersected, and superseded each other. The music of the gypsy orchestras included the violin, viola, cello, double bass, clarinet, and cimbalom. Gypsy orchestra music also was recorded to have lead troops into battle at times. Real gypsy folk music used no instruments. Instead stamping feet, clicking tongues, the tapping of spoons, and the rapping of knuckles on tables accompanied real gypsy singers.

Rosa's mother played the harp and most wonderfully too. The music was dreamlike and on many occasions she would woo Rosa to sleep when on their travels in the summer holidays. Experiences never to be forgotten embedded in Rosa's heart and soul. Mingling with life and customs, music was part of gypsy folk law and Rosa would dance and swirl around the camp fire on summer sultry nights. This was her heritage and she embraced it with enthusiasm. Randy, Rosa's father played the accordion.

There was always music available, tambourines, congas, violins, mandolins, guitars. Music was the life blood of the gypsies.

If you imagined this to be Rosa, then you would not be far off in your guestimation. The idea here is to give a valued look and feel to the aspects of gypsy life, and to the essence that resides in the heart of their ways and culture. Rosa depicts this fundamental part of their nature in spirit, principles and substance.

Throughout the world, Romani (or Gypsy) musicians and dancers are gifted and inspired artists, honoring individuality, creative talent and personal expression. The arts of music and dance of the Roma range from India to the famously provocative Flamenco Puro to the haunting beauty of Eastern European music and the French Django Rinehart and "Gypsy Jazz".

More than a technique, it is personal style and attitude which makes music and dance distinctly Roma. For the Rom, the arts of music and dance are an expression of emotion, placing high value on improvisation, intensity, and originality. The Romani arts, including Flamenco, act as a system for teaching and claiming cultural history and serves as a collective healing. Romani music and dance is, at its peak, an expression of talent and sublimation. It is a manner of enduring and transcending life's emotional repertoire of sorrow, grief and pain.

HISTORY OF THE GYPSY/ROMA

Diverse, nomadic . . . to be Roman or "gypsy," is to be a member of an ethnic minority that is difficult to define in any definite, factual terms. Throughout their history, the Roma have been comprised of many different groups of people, absorbing outsiders and other cultures while migrating across continents. This has resulted in creating a patchwork of groups calling themselves Roma, Romani, Romany or Gypsy, each with a differing culture customs, and now in only the current times—written languages.

Despite their differences, the Roma do share certain attributes. Made up of four "tribes," or nations (natsiya), they are bound together at least through Rom blood and Romani (or Romanes), the root language they share. The Roma also hold common characteristics: they are extremely loyal to family and clan; a strong belief in both Del (God) and Beng (the Devil); belief in predestiny; and Romaniya, loosely translated as certain standards and norms in codes of conduct (which vary in degree from tribe to tribe). At their core, because of their history, they are people who are adaptable to changing conditions.

Gypsy Travellers have a long history in Britain and modern Gypsy culture is the product of many influences but its roots reach back as far as ninth century India.

Kent has historically had a high population of Gypsy Travellers because the fruit and vegetable farms in the Garden of England needed a large mobile workforce, providing Travellers with an ideal way of making a living.

In horse drawn days the extended family would travel and work together following a seasonal pattern of work on the county's farms. In winter time they would pull on to one of the traditional stopping places on the edges of towns.

In the years after the second world war the work gradually dried up and increasing legislation made stopping places harder to find. Eventually most Gypsies had to give up the traveling life and settle down.

In modern times Gypsy Travellers are having to adapt an ancient culture which was developed and sustained through traveling into a sedentary existence.

That it has survived this far is testimony to the tenacity of the Romany people and there is little doubt that it will be around for a long time yet.

Making a living

Kent, The Garden of England, with its concentration of fruit and vegetable farms relied on the Travellers to provide temporary seasonal labour. They were an essential part of the local agricultural workforce.

The annual round of farm work began in late spring with hop training and throughout the summer and autumn Gypsey Travellers moved from farm to farm as each crop needed harvesting.

Cherries, strawberries, blackcurrants during high summer as well as peas, beans and other vegetables were needed to be quickly gathered in as they ripened.

The hops were ready in September followed by apples and pears in the autumn and potato picking up in early winter.

They might stay on for a while after picking finished on one farm before moving on to the next, perhaps breaking their journey with overnight stops on commons.

Places like Yalding Lees or Hothfield Common near Ashford were traditional stopping places where Gypsy families might stop for a day or two before moving on.

During the winter months most local Travellers would find a place to stop on the edge of the larger towns or the urban fringes of south east London where there were large traditional stopping places that had been used by Travellers for generations.

Ash Tree Lane in Chatham was one such place, as were the marshes along the Thames at Erith, the disused chalk pit at Ruxley near Sidcup and Corke's Meadow in St. Mary Cray.

Winter money could be earned by making and selling wooden clothes pegs, primrose baskets or decorative wooden flowers from door to door. Men could find casual labouring work.

Settling down

Much of the traditional farm work gradually disappeared after the end of the Second World War due to increasing mechanization and agrochemical farming methods.

By the mid 1960s all hops were picked by machines and herbicides had dispensed with the need for hand weeding. Gradually the fruit farms that still needed extra labour at harvest time were beginning to employ students from abroad rather than the Travellers and other local people.

During this period Travellers continued to resort to their traditional over wintering sites on the edges of major urban settlements where some casual employment could be gained.

As the farm work dried up, so did the impetus to keep traveling and the winter stop overs gradually became large permanent settlements.

The nomadic life was further hampered by successive legislation aimed at preventing roadside stopping and caravan dwelling.

With decreasing work and the increasing harassment, many families gradually stopped pulling down into Kent to follow the work and remained permanently on the winter stopping places near towns. Many eventually made the move from caravans and trailers on these sites into nearby houses.

Rosa actually lived part of her life in a caravan. What I mean by "caravan" is as is known in the present climate as mobile home (on wheels), a prestigious mobile home with all its amenities and attributes.

Rosa's father was a prize fighter and known throughout the land, he was a romany with the name of his forbears stamped impeccable on his chest and in his heart. Prize fighting to this day is a big money spinner and Randy (knuckles) St. Clare was one of the best, renowned all over as far as Europe's towns and cities.

Crystal St. Clare (Rosa's mother) was a dark skinned attractive woman with arms like a man, but sensual none the less. She did have the gift of clairvoyance but not on the scale of her mother, Rosa's grandmother, who would sell her wears and tears along with a little fortune telling. Money was never scarce in the St. Clare family. Land leases, stocks and shares, jewelry, precious heir looms locked in the vaults of major banks in London and New York. These secrets and treasures were held in esteem and confidentiality by her age defying mother in a quaint thatched cottage in north east Cornwall.

Through the decades of travel and the ongoing nomadic lifestyle money and property and riches were accumulated and passed down to the descendants of the St. Clare brethren. Rosa was one of the last descendants and all would be passed down to her and or her family in due course. One of the items that was sold off was a pristine mobile home.

Over a period of time the living quarters of the St. Clare household was renewed and up dated. Rosa's father died of a brain hemorrhage. The money he had amassed from his prize fighting in later years (cage fighting) was astronomical. From the sale of the prestigious state of the art home on wheels, Crystal, Rosa's mother raised seventy five thousand pounds. Her days of roaming were over. This payment became a wedding present on Glen and Rosa's magical day. Along with Rosslyn they had no money worries. The deeds to Rosslyn were passed over by Glen's father. A hand shake and a hug, was the order of the day. Just the up keep and the maintenance was all Glen had to worry about.

In August 1973—the backdrop for a prestigious shoot aimed at the tartan dress and culture was located at the annual Edinburgh Military

Tattoo. Permission was granted by the local authorities. It lasted most of the day, dozens of photos were taken, locations and sets were assembled at different sites around Edinburgh Castle. The Scots Guards were present and were performing with their pipes and drums. Glen was part of the occasion and was playing the bagpipes.

Later in the evening after their part in the show (The Tattoo) the brigade relaxed in the confines of the castle and its grounds.

This was the chance the model agency was waiting for, the realism of the event. The idea was to capture the natural essence of the Military Celebrations. The photographer was a little camp. The sixties and the seventies were still a little shy about feminine types and homosexuality. Gays were not openly active in the mainstream of things. But if you were in the fashion, art and design, you could blend in with the avant-garde persona and be accepted without too much hoo-ha or raising of eyebrows.

"Darling that's fabulous!" Robin would say maneuvering his zoom lens camera this way and that, angling for the best shot panning wildly. "Eyes darling, eyes, please flutter those eye lashes, soulful now, now wild, now windswept, more blowers please!" he would shout to his assistants. "More wind in the hair, chin up dear!" he would say.

Rosa would comply, she loved the attention really. With two years study behind her she was now a professional.

Glen was passing with his comrades. "Shall we do one more shot?" Robin said very effeminately. "Oh excuse me sir, would you please just stand there for a moment, Rosa, just there darling, one more shot with the soldier behind". Glen stood not blinking an eye, but there was an affinity, a realization love was in the air. "Oh darling, he's gorgeous, that uniform". Robin brushed his eyebrow with the tips of his forefinger and middle finger in a dramatic swirling swooning motion then hands on hips he gestured Rosa to move closer.

"Nonchalant dear, nonchalant, wonderful, wonderful!" Robin expressed with flicking flailing hands. Camera resting by it's leather strap over his shoulders and against his breast plate. "Finished! Finished! break everyone, coffee tea, thank you!"

"And your name is?" Robin spoke to Glen. Rosa was fixing her hair, straightening her dress. With his limp hands Robin gently sidled the two of them together. Rosa had never seen this side of life. All these six foot plus handsome men in their sparkling attire standing to attention regimental and pristine. "Glen Barrington of her Majesties armed forces the Scots Guards!" he pronounced proudly. "Well thank you Glen" said Robin flabbergasted. "And this is Rosa!" announced Robin, palms open and down gesturing to his favourite prodigy. "One of our best models and a valued member of our staff!".

Glen bowed with a nod of his head. "Rosa!" Glen said in admiration of her fine alluring presence and enchantment. Enthralled with each other their eyes met in a blaze of attraction. "I hope we meet again". "I hope so too" replied Rosa. They parted, their heart melting with passion. "My God she's a vision" said one of his compatriots, "You must get her number or find out how to get in touch". Glen had a plan, he would not lose her.

The Royal Edinburgh Military Tattoo is an annual series of Military tattoos performed by British Armed Forces, Commonwealth and International military bands and display teams in the Scottish capital Edinburgh. The event takes place annually throughout August, as part of the wider Edinburgh Festival (a collective name for many independent festivals and events in Edinburgh in August).

The word "Tattoo" is derived from "Doe den tap toe", or just "tap toe" ("toe is pronounced "too"), the Dutch for "Last orders". Translated literally, it means: "put the tap to", or "close or turn off the tap". The term "Tap-toe" was first encountered by the British Army when stationed in Flanders during the War of the Austrian Succession.

The British adopted the practice and it became a signal, played by a regiment's Corps of Drums or Pipes and Drums each night to tavern owners to turn off the taps of their ale kegs so that the soldiers would retire to their billeted lodgings at a reasonable hour. With the establishment of modern barracks and full Military bands later in the 18th century, the term Tattoo was used to describe not only the last duty call of the day, but also a ceremonial form of evening entertainment performed by Military musicians.

Although the first Tattoo in Edinburgh, entitled "Something About a Soldier", took place at the Ross Bandstand at Princes Street Gardens in 1949, the first official Edinburgh Military Tattoo began in 1950 with just eight items in the programme. It drew some 6000 spectators seated in simple bench and scaffold structures around the north, south and east sides of the Edinburgh Castle esplanade. In 1952, the capacity of the stands was increased to accommodate a nightly audience of 7700, allowing 160,000 to watch live performances each year.

Now, on average, just over 217,000 people see the Tattoo live on the esplanade of Edinburgh Castle each year, and it has sold out in advance of the last decade. 30% of the audience are from Scotland and 35% from the rest of the United Kingdom. The remaining 35% of the audience consists of 70,000 visitors from overseas. Only the Edinburgh Festival Fringe is a bigger part of the Edinburgh Festival, although that consists of over 2,000 productions staged across 247 venues. The current temporary Grandstands on the castle esplanade were first used in 1975 and have a capacity of 8600.

The town was alive the hustle and bustle of the tourists, the music of every kind, the pageantry of the festival. The lights, the Castle lit up in all it's glory. The Scottish brogue, the tartan cloth. The marching bands. The Majesty of the moment. The multicoloured spectacle of the performance enhancing the aura that permeated the city.

Dusk was forming, it was now twilight. Robin thanked Glen for his help and handed him a business card and promised to send him a personalised portfolio of the shoot. Two weeks passed by and in the post came an A4 sized folder complete with pictorial images of the day. Etched in gold leaf print was a thank you card with the company's name and address. This was Glens chance, a lifeline to Rosa. An omen a portent to romantic liaisons. He now had a link, a reason to make contact. He would ring the agency and find out Rosa's number and call.

His justification for contacting her would be to congratulate her on the fine work she had produced during her stay in Scotland and at the Edinburgh Military Tattoo. The photos would be the main talking point. "I was pleased with the photographs that were sent to the head quarters (R.H.Q.) London". "As I was Glen, as I was" replied Rosa. "I enjoyed myself so much and was very pleased to have met you".

Glen spoke again "I was wondering if you would care to take a tour of Edinburgh and the highlands if you have time to spare. My family would be honored if you accepted and you would be welcome to stay at the ancestral home for the duration. Please say yes!"

"Yes" said Rosa instantly and emphatically. "I would love to". Glen was elated.

Rosa was twenty one years of age at this time. Glen was twenty four. They'd both had minor skirmishes of a carnal nature. Close encounters of a sexual kind, but nothing on the scale of major love making, actual full blooded head on fornication. Glen was a little shy in his early years. Rosa was a little choosy and had never met anyone that she could take into her heart. Accidents can de-flower a young girl in her adolescence. 1973 was an awakening of permissive attitudes. Many teenagers from the sixties onward had a succession of lovers. But there was still that air of decency and protocol concerning sexuality and promiscuity. An element of propriety persisted a conformity to the prevailing standards of behaviour.

Along with the selection of snapshots there was also a brochure/ catalogue for a company that dealt with the manufacture of such fashion. The introduction read as follows;

Ladies Tartarn Kilts & Skirts from Scotland!
A Genuine Scottish Tartan kilt—to complete your wardrobe!

We provide a wide range of ladies' kilts as well as long and short tartan skirts which we have available in a comprehensive selection of Scottish wove clan tartans. To complement both casual and informal outfits we have designed and produced very attractive corsets in various tartans which can be used to great effect with our evening and wedding dresses or to spice up a simple casual outfit. To accessorise we also have tartan shawls, capes, ponchos and handbags which will create a tasteful accent for any everyday formal or casual outfit. We also stock a collection of casual clothes with an accent and touch of Scotland which will give the wearer a subtle and stylish Scottish air.

Rosa felt that traveling by car from her home in Truro would be a major treck. This was her leisure time. She always took time off in late August/September and staying with Glen in Scotland was ideal. Glen and his father would be waiting at the platform on her arrival.

The Cosy family lodge was bedecked with rambling roses, geraniums pink, white and purple, grew in a multitude around the threshold. Rosa hugged her mother with a fine embrace that showed care and understanding. She waved and closed the white picket fence gate. A taxi took Rosa to Falmouth train station to board a sleeper. The two day trip was a little arduous but comfortable. The book she chose for the excursion up to Waverly Station in Edinburgh was Lady Chatterley's Lover by D. H. Lawrence. A thing she would never admit to Glen concerning her reading material, for the time being anyway.

The journey in itself was a realization of dedication to the call of romance, an "affaire de Coeur".

Glen spoke as they sauntered into the town. "Let me reimburse you for your traveling expenses". "Glen," Rosa haltered her step. "I earn twenty thousand pounds a year, and I'm on my vacation. It's my choice to come to Scotland".

They walked on. Glen smiled tight lipped and admired her even more in that one exchange of discourse. An understanding, an infusion, a perception about the kind of woman he had brought into his world. "We'll say no more on the subject" Glen replied secretly loving her tenacity.

It was hot that day, with a cool Scottish breeze. The smell of the North Sea freshened the sinuses wafting in from the Firth of Forth. Glen in kharki shorts, t-shirt and blue cloth covered plimsoles. Rosa in red hot pants and a cream high necked long sleeved vest that hugged her desirable figure. Block heeled cream shoes strapped up to the knees complimented a large psychedelic carpet bag that hung over her shoulder and onto her hip. Her usual beads and bangles swayed and jangled as she strolled on, like a pretty flamingo. A rose tattoo was painted onto her left cheekbone. Her hair like golden fleece shone in the sunlight. Held in place by a plastic red band she was a child of the Universe. An icon to the seventies and the age of Aquarius.

So called "The Athens of the North", Edinburgh has a wealth of interest bubbling away at its core. The Royal Mile, Princes St and its well known shopping area. The Castle, St. Giles Cathedral. Princess St. Gardens, Sir Walter Scott's monument. The winding streets. The fascinating lanes and alleys.

After the short tour meandering the streets of the town, Rosa and Glen sat in a secluded café looking directly up to the Castle. Glen was browsing through the catalogue. Glen's father had left his son and his new found acquaintance and returned to the estate in Midlothian along with Rosa's luggage.

"Rosa, you look so good in that tartan basque". Glen thought it a little risqué for a woman's clothes mag. "I will get it framed for you Glen and maybe I could wear it for you one day, we are given the clothes that we model free of charge, I hardly buy my own since I became a model". "I would like that Rosa" Glen said, with a gleam in his eye. He looked at her and she at him, their eyes locked in unison and they kissed passionately and in hunger of each others need and intensity for the love they ultimately knew was in their hearts. A blinding love, that tore at their very souls. A spontaneous release of true affection.

That night at the grand cottage in it's ten acres of land covered in bracken and heather spinnys and coppices, the pan tile styled roof glinting in the moonlight, mist resting on it's surface like a phosphorous glow. The highlands sweeping down to the lowlands. The craggy rocks and mountains away in the distance. Edinburgh Castle just visible several miles away on it's hilltop. The real romantism of the Scottish scenery shouting out it's glory and shades of the mystic past.

An all night lantern beamed out across the landscape from the forecourt. Bare chested and in his pyjama bottoms, Glen with his leather slip on night shoes that fell silently on to the solid wood floors in the hallway crept furtively across to Rosa's room.

Rosa was naked except for a red lacy pair of camisole panties. A light cotton sheet barely covered her hot nubile body. The door was unlocked, she felt it was a safe environment especially with Glen only feet away down the hall. In fact there was a secret hope that Glen in covert clandestine shades of night would take her in his arms and make erotic rousing wild sex to her desperately wanting libido. Her eyes gently closed, her soft fragrant hair resting against the large white pillows, she felt a little vulnerable but comfortable and secure. The door opened easy and silently. Her eyes flickered slightly at the change in temperature and the essence of movement in the room. Her eye lids heavy and partially open, she visualized Glen. His torso gleaming from the low light in the lobby as he quietly closed the door over. She lifted the sheet from her nakedness as Glen clambered in. Their bodies met in adoration and consent for the moment at hand.

The lovemaking was unique not earth shattering but amorous and adoring. Their flesh harmonizing into one heated exchange of cohesion. A shimmering act of intimacy, delight, and a tenderness that can only be imagined as a heavenly aura surrounded by a golden ambience. The stroking of hips, legs, arms, hair, faces. Kisses were applied to every part of their anatomy. Palms of the hands finding all the erogenous zones. Carefully exploring all the crevices and the tender regions leaving no room for unattended feelings. The slow and deliberate movement of their actions. The removal of flimsy underwear discarded with care and delicacy letting it drop to the floor of the bedroom. Completely naked, now lips on lips, Rosa's legs entwined with Glens. Glen's tender thrust penetrating Rosa's moist and willing warm like vaginal opening. They were now one for ever. True love now cemented in a celebrated and elevated existence of ecstacy.

The next morning Rosa arose with a glorious tint to her cheeks. The Scottish air, the amorous passions that still reverberated through her system was invigorating as the fresh morning dew that glistened on the windswept heaths surrounding the small holding. A cottars residence now upgraded from a gaels (Scottish Highlanders) humble home to a seventeen century pristine domain consisting of a five bedroom house/

cottage with stables, a barn, double garages, housing a four by four Mitzzubishi shogun, and a red 1960 E-type Jaguar in a mint condition. Cattle grassed in the fields that were fenced off by three by two inch beams of teak. A dirt track led the way to a perfectly cobbled courtyard. Great black shiny doors with massive brass door handles graced verd antique stone steps, leading to the entrance. This was the landscape of Bonny Rigg near Roslin and its famous Castle and Chapel.

The legend steeped in the hearts and minds of the locals that was enriched by its auspicious history and divine vibrations.

The courtship continued through the years. Glen and Rosa were in contact with each other up to five times a year. Sometimes Glen would travel to Cornwall and Rosa to Scotland. Sometimes London or whatever city they would be working or stationed in. He with his unit, Rosa with the model agency.

Love never relinquished it's power to reunite, to embellish, to accommodate. The future was already at hand. Destiny wrapped itself around their ever increasing devotion and affection. The lovable attachment that would never die. Blended into an association that blossomed into stark realism and ever lasting union.

Glen and Rosa honeymooned in Europe and on their travels they included the journey of the seven chakras as show on the map below.

The builders of these great cathedrals deliberately erected them on Druidic sites, dedicated to the planetary oracles.

Glen could speak Spanish. Rosa could speak French, two of the things that made their journey less arduous. Not that it was difficult or demanding. It wasn't quite a back packing holiday, but there would be times when the terrain and driving and commuting would be very demanding. Rosa owned a mini cooper, not the most comfortable car on the road. But then they were young, brave, resilient and free. This was an adventure not to be missed.

Glen was organised. Rosa was a woman of the world and had travelled extensively in her job. The combination and the love they shared would conquer all. They had given themselves six weeks to complete their mission. Their first priority was full comprehensive insurance for themselves and the vehicle. Personal medical cover and breakdown service finances would be completely structured to their needs.

The innocence of the day, the greeness of England, the pure sunshine and the blue skies of Spain. The quaintness and beauty of France, the food, the wine, the locals and their ways. The music, the enchantment, things were different then. The aura of the 60's and 70's was all consuming. There was a spirit of freedom. No restrictions, open roads, free love, adventure was in the air. Ideas and the courage of youth abounded. Money would be deposited at each of the towns on their journey through the seven druidic sites. They would carry travellers cheques, maybe a little change. Pesos and francs.

Glen's army influence and Rosa's knowledge of customs and geography would be vital in their quest. This was not to be some bizarre religious act. It was a personal odyssey. An expedition to find their true faith, to consolidate their belief in the All Mighty. To believe, to be enlightened. To build a monument to the glory of God. To seal their vows. They were fun loving and loved life. This was a combination of fact and fulfilment, fantasy and fascination.

First they would drive to Portsmouth, collect the Ferry and on to Santander in North West Spain where they had booked their hotel. This was also a bonding of their love. They would make love on each visit to the sacred oracles. This is what they promised themselves. It was after all their honeymoon.

Love is essential in matters of the heart and spirit, and love they did. It was all consuming and erotic, Glen could not get enough of Rosa, and Rosa he. They would make love for hours. Rosa climaxed time and time again. Glen taking his body to heights of ecstasy, almost exhausting his libido taking it beyond human endurance.

On lazy summer days the sun would beam through the windows of their accommodation, be it a grand hotel or a quaint bed and breakfast or a cottage for two, an inn or a hostel, lying naked tanned, radiant with health and vitality, almost worshiping each other on their bed, be it grand or unpretentious, the wine and champagne flowing, the romantic restaurants, the exotic walks on the beach, the moonlight nights in each others arms kissing passionately taking in the horizon and the setting sun. Watching the glorious dazzling spectacular views and then gazing into each others eyes with openness and complete devotion. But the main strategy was the adoration of the seven oracles to combine, to worship an inner spirit, to integrate, to find peace and tranquillity within. There was never a word of animosity. Never a falling out. Never a desertion, only light hearted scolding or playful banter. This would be the blue print for eternity, for their eternity. There was an easiness, a trust if you believe in horoscopes.

Then Glen, was a Gemini, Rosa a Libran, the seventh sign of the zodiac. The sun is in this sign between about 23rd September and 22nd October. Gemini is the third sign of the zodiac. The sun is in this sign between about 21st May and 20th June. An infusion I believe that created a supernova affect. Two giant stars coming together blending into one giant nuclear explosion of celestial love, passion and devotion.

The sex in the earlier days was amazing. Some of the carnal positions that Glen would have Rosa in, a contortionist would have trouble with. But Rosa loved her man. She did not particularly enjoy the doggy style, as people so crudely put it "from behind" seems more appropriate. She liked to look at her lover when she was making love, to see his face and gaze into his eyes. But she would accept little quirks of that nature if they occurred during their sexual romps.

Glen was a strong young man of twenty seven. Rosa was a virginal beauty of twenty four. Her hair and eyes I've spoken about. But in her youth she had everything a man could want. Her porcelain chin complimented her high cheekbones. The slightly turned up nose, a perfection of symmetry. Her breasts firm and tender to the touch. At 5 feet 5 inches she was slender and sexy. Her neck was swan like. Every inch of her body was a glorification of vitality. The heart shaped rear, the long shapely legs. The seductive pout of her reddened lips. They never really changed. They still have that glow and effectiveness about them. Glen's strong will and Rosa's feminine charms. Glen's athletic build and charisma, his handsomeness never faded. Rosa's lady like airs and graces. She did have a wild side and would be first to strip at a beach party and go skinny dipping. Glen was a little more reserved. But he loved her spirituality. She could probably drink him under the table if it ever came to that. The way Rosa looked in a pair of well washed, worn and torn denims was a sight for sore eyes. Sometimes bra-less in a v-neck t-shirt or a silk blouse, "absolutely stunning" is the phrase.

They shared the driving most days, and Rosa would be seen with her head raised; chin up taking in the countryside. Regal and proud and happy that her beau (husband) was at the helm, sharing this adventure. Glen would glance her way. Rosa would turn her head and their thoughts would melt into an infusion in the knowledge that they were one and in each others care and protection. An assurance, a belief, a bond, a dedication to belong to sustain to harnish the relationship of something magical and everlasting. There were no sat navs and Tom-Toms. Maps and common sense ruled the day. It was fun stopping on route asking for directions if they were unsure. It was relaxed. If they were tired or needed a break they would search out a B & B and rest for the night, there was no hurry.

This was life on a roll. Their belongings piled high on the roof rack. The red Mini Cooper, a tough fairly comfortable little motor car, zoomed up and down motorways and A roads. They would stop at roadsides, country lanes, hill tops surveying the scenery. Picnicking on the grass. People would wave and smile their way, it was like that in the seventies. There was an air of welcome camaraderie, the age of the flower power. The innocence of the day unhindered carefree.

Sometimes Rosa would paint flowers on her cheekbones and neck. A true sixties wild child. Rings and beads brightly coloured with semi precious stones hung from her shoulders and shone on her hands. Jade, Opal, Turquoise, Amber, Topaz. A beautiful Gold table cut brooch was worn for special days out. Amassed with citrine at it's centre, it was surrounded by gems of every type. Amethyst, Garnet, Aquamarine, Agate, Tigers Eye Pearl. It was a fabulous piece of jewellery that Rosa adored. She was the epitome of the sexual revolution. The age of Aquarius, freedom and love. She was all empowering and Glen was swept away with the splendour of it all. She was almost gypsy-like with gold and silver bracelets, jingling and jangling upon her delicate feminine wrists.

Her flared multi coloured skirt and loose camisole top, the red slim fitting ballet shoes, the black velvet band which held her hair in place. Told of a flitting nymph on glorious summer days, the hazy sunshine adding to the charm and mystique of the moment Glen was robust, tall and lithe. His dark brown hair was thick, full and touching his collar. He was relaxed and a long way from his army duties, content with his new found independence and life on the road. Passing from Scotland through England then onto Spain was a mixture of pleasant lands, lochs, meadows, landscapes of immeasurable beauty of endless shades of green. Rivers, lakes, forests, swallows swooping here and there in the endless blue skies above. The fresh air, those enchanting summer months those golden sandy beaches of Spain. The quaintness of France. The thatched cottages of England. The heather and the bracken of Scotland. The white walled adobes in Spanish towns. The cosmopolitan cafes and bars of the French villages, tables on the pavements serving wine and coffee. The cars and buses honking and beeping on the narrow winding streets. The garcons with their silver trays and white aprons serving the hordes of suntanned tourists. The French bread, the cheese, the locals on their bikes, onions slung over their shoulders, whistling with their berets on and distinct handlebar moustaches. The Gendarmes watching every move. The cathedrals magnificent in their ornate splendour. A monument to the glorification of God and the Heavens built by the ancient world. The masons of the era portraying their vast knowledge of art and décor perfected through the ages. For the edification of future societies. The proof that God's immediate and undying love lives within stone and masonry, bricks and mortar, marble and granite.

Rosslyn Chapel is relatively small, at 40' 8" high, 34' 8" wide, and 68' long.

The arched stone ceiling of Rosslyn Chapel is finely decorated in squares with five pointed stars, ball flowers, tablet flowers, roses, a dove with an olive branch.

Seashells are found next to a carving of Sir William, which are the symbol of St. James. Together with the stars on the ceiling, they may represent Santiago da Compostela ("St. James of the Field of Stars").

Throughout the Rosslyn Chapel are many fleur-de-lis designs. This may suggest the work of artists from France, but the fleur-de-lis is also associated with the Virgin Mary as well as with royalty.

On the three pillars standing between the east aisle and the east chapel is a choir of 13 angels with musical instruments, representing the host of God. On the ribs of the intersections on the north and south sides are representations of various occupations in life, referred to as the "Dance of Death."

Carvings on other pillars include Issac on the altar with the ram, Abraham looking towards his son, Samson destroying the Philistines, David killing the lion, the Prodigal son, the Crucifixion, and scenes from the history of the Roslin Family. Also of interest are the masons' marks on the individual stones, the use of which was rare at the time of building.

Rosslyn Chapel is the home of the famous Apprentice Pillar, a decorated pillar that gets its name from a legend involving the mason in charge of the stonework in the chapel and his young apprentice.

According to the legend, the master mason felt he needed to see the original inspiration for the design, located in Rome, before he could perform the complicated task of carving the column. But upon his return, he found that his upstart apprentice had completed the column. In a fit of jealous rage, the mason struck the apprentice on the head and killed him. The head of the unlucky apprentice is depicted in a corner opposite the organ loft, complete with a scar on his left temple.

The base of the Apprentice Pillar depicts eight dragons, from whose mouths emerge the vine that winds itself around the pillar. In Christian mythology, this represents the Tree of Life, but it probably was inspired by Norse mythology (perhaps due to Rosslyn Chapel's founder's connection with Orkney). The Norse Tree of Knowledge, Yggdrasil, holds up the heavens from the earth and the dragons of time gnaw at the roots of the Tree.

Near the Apprentice Pillar is a Latin inscription that reads, "Wine is strong, a king is stronger, women are stronger still, but truth conquers all." The text comes from the apocryphal book of Esdras.

There exists a chapel in Great Britain that contains a ceiling from which hundreds of stone blocks protrude, jutting down to form a bizarre multi-faceted surface. Each block is carved with a symbol, seemingly at random, creating a cipher of unfathomable proportion. Modern cryptographers have never been able to break this code, and a generous reward is offered to anyone who can decipher the baffling message.

In recent years, geological ultrasounds have revealed the startling presence of an enormous subterranean vault hidden beneath the chapel. This vault appears to have no entrance and no exit. To this day, the curators of the chapel have permitted no excavation.

Recently, researchers and Grail enthusiasts have been probing into the historical Rosslyn Chapel to determine once and for all if this is truly the house of the Cup of Christ. Researchers using the latest scanning, MRI, and Ultrasonic technologies, plan to view under the ground to attempt to locate the "secret vaults" preset inside.

Quick Facts

Site Information

Names:	Rosslyn Chapel; Roslin Chapel; Collegiate Church of St Matthew
Location:	Lothian, Scotland
Faith:	Christianity
Denomination:	Original/Primary: Catholic
	Current/Secondary: Scottish Episcopal
Dedication:	St. Matthew
Category:	Churches
Status:	active
Date:	1446
Patron:	Sir William Sinclair
Architecture:	Gothic

Rosa and Glen did not need the guidance of a teacher to attain the illumination. They believed in their heart and soul that their true feelings and dedication to the veneration of the seven oracles was embedded in the very depths of their souls. They would conduct their own path to the enlightenment and contentment, hand in hand. The Lord's prayer was a great example. Their own thoughts and wishes combined with the power of prayer and meditation. Light hearted, relaxed, contemplative, absorbing the ambiance of each of the sites.

A natural carefree exposition of the teaching that correspond to seven sacred chakras. The journey itself releasing endorphins and adrenaline. The pure sunlight, the exotic air. The combination of adventure and experiences. The thrill and stimulation of living day to day. Enthusiastic, awakening the emotions transforming the basic feeling into sensations of awareness, sense and sensibility at it's peak.

As they travelled each chakra in the body would be opened to their own realisation and they would abide by the rules, facts and details within the laws and regulations of pilgrimage. The magnificence of the great cathedrals would invoke wonder and celebrations. The aura that resides in each of the sacred symbols. The work, the art that went into building such monumental structures. The love and dedication that was instilled within the stonemasons and craftsmen of the day. A shrine, a testament to God's immaculate power. A token of reverence here on earth. An umbilical cord to Heaven's maternal abode. They gained solace in the confines of each cathedral, soaking up the atmosphere, living the dream. Fortifying each energy centre that relates to every divination on the sacred path of enlightenment. Dwelling in those hallows halls. The musty smell, the light through the stained glass decorative windows. The stone walls, the majesty of its unique form and grandeur. The holiness, the silence and solitude, the peacefulness, enhancing the pure level of spirituality and righteousness. The element of religion is vast. It's all consuming there's a need for comfort and faith within the realms of human existence and it's a consolidation. A reinforcement, a fortification, a stabilization. The very essence of natural fulfilment, it's an obligation to a higher energy but there's also the guarantee of the presence within society. A pledge to justify a living a common process, an undertaking that persists and resides in the bosom.

They were tourists after all. They were human, mortal. They lived in another era. One could drink on a massive scale and commute by car and not consider the importance or dangers lurking therein. Now it's hardly a pint or a glass of wine.

Rosa would organise lunch boxes, drinks, wine. A glass of wine while driving never killed anyone I imagine but Glen and Rosa never over did the alcoholic measures. There was a natural caring and consideration for the planet as a whole. Holidaying was quiet, sombre relaxing. The thought of being reckless or irresponsible was out of the question. She was so womanly and thoughtful. Her queen like ways complemented Glen's princely manner and select attitude towards life and living. She knew his likes and dislikes and in the same essence he would grant her almost anything that was in his power.

They took photographs on special occasions. Fun loving acting, teasing, posing, Rosa was a natural. A camcorder was brought out of it's case when the moment was right. Sometimes Glen would catch Rosa in her rollers or when her features were white with its face pack. She would run and hide with Glen in frivolous pursuit on the beach in her bikini and floppy hat. Catching her with a fork full of spaghetti, eating a slice of water melon, an ice cream cornet. Applying her lipstick, "Glen", she would say sternly "That's enough!".

She would recap the stick in it's tube, press and roll her lips and then pout. Check in the mirror, pull at the strands of her fine chiffon shoulder length hair. Run her fingers over the eyebrows, straighten the collar of her crimson red blouse, reset the pearl necklace she was wearing (a present from Glen), no reason just a present. She would smile "Ready!", she would say. Her feminine wiles brimming with enchantment. Clasping her purse and looping her arm around Glen's they would stroll out into the Spanish sunshine or meander the streets of France. Perusing, contemplating, consummating their time on earth. Glen was enthralled. Rosa was radiant, a magnificence, an infusion in the spectrum of life. Alchemy working its magical spell.

Glen in white oxford bags, brown open toe sandals, a brown leather belt and a beige cheesecloth short sleeved shirt. Rosa's white flared skirt and bare tanned legs blended with her red comfy ballet shoes. They were a picture to see. These were the moments they cherished. Time after time these moments of spontaneity cemented their amour. Glen sometimes would rest his arm over her shoulders, his other hand in his trouser pocket. So relaxed in her company she would kiss his cheek. On this day, Rosa threw her arms around Glen's waist "You know", she said "Mum told me I'd marry an army man and be happy for the rest of my existence, you're that man Glen, my man!". "Rosa!" Glen said softly and gently. "I adore you, you're an angel and I'll never let you go!". They kissed so passionately that sparks of electricity permeated the warm, sultry, exotic air. Their bodies embraced in an emotional cocoon of love.

They loved in sweet surrender and how they loved. It was a coming together, actually coming together that is. "Climaxing" happened on each visit to the sacred sites. They would endeavour to create that sensation. It became a natural event. Concentration was vital in meeting of the senses in the consummation and completion of sexual perfection. Totally enthralled with love and loving they would hold on gazing into each other's eyes in heavenly raptures of ecstasy, studying each others movements and looks, eyes wide with enchanting glances, breathing heavily holding on for that single moment when two would be one. All consuming angelic loving. They made it happen time and time again panting, moaning, giggling with the thrill of it all. Cries of delight ringing in the air. Two alone for a single throne. Their hot trembling lips would meet, they would caress and stroke, kiss and hug and then sleep.

Santiago de Compostela Cathedral of St. James de Compostela was the first visit. Everything in this world is based on the nucleus of religion and the exposition, description, illustration, interpretation and heavenly account of Christianity, from the very moment Adam and Eve graced this fertile planet. Glen and Rosa would initiate the base chakra "survival". They had made the decision to live and strive for harmony and not succumb to negative vibes or stresses. Their outlook was a happy and confident one, to exist without barriers of restrictions. They would fight for themselves and for the future they hoped and wished would be strong and secure through hard work, and a structured purpose for life on earth.

Santiago, in full Santiago de Compostela city, La Coruna provincia in the comunidad autonoma ("autonomous community") of Galicia, north-western Spain near the confluence of the Sar and Sarela rivers, 32 miles (51km) southwest of La Coruna city. Santiago is the Spanish for St. James, whose shrine the city possesses. In AD 813 a tomb discovered at nearby Padron was said to have been supernaturally revealed to be that of the apostle St. James the Great, martyred at Jerusalem in about AD 44. His bones had been taken to Spain, where according to legend, he had formerly evangelized. The discovery of the relics provided a rallying point for Christian Spain, then confined to a narrow strip at the north of the Iberia peninsula, most of which was occupied by Moors. Over the tomb Alfonso II of Asturias built an earthen church that Alfonso III replaced by a stone one, and the town that grew up around it became the most important Christian place of pilgrimage after Jerusalem and Rome during the Middle Ages. The whole town, except the tomb itself, was destroyed in 997 by Abu Air al-Mansur (Almanzor), military commander of the Moorish caliphate of Cordoba. In 1078 the present cathedral was begun by order of Alfonso VI of Leon and Castile. This Romanesque building (consecrated 112, completed 1211), located at the east end of the Plaza Mayor, has a Baroque west façade (El Obradoiro) above a flight of steps, built by Fernando Casas y Novoa (1738-47). An outstanding feature of the interior is the Portico de la Gloria (located behind the façade), a tripartite porch showing a Last Judgement, Romanesque but tinged with Gothic features by Maestro Mateo. At the north of the Plaza Mayor is the Hospice of the Catholic Kings (Hospicio de los Reyes Catolicos), built in 501-11 by Enrique de Egas to receive the pilgrims and later used as a hotel. Other noteworthy secular buildings are the colleges of San Jeronimo (founded 1501). Fonseca (founded 1530) and San Clemente (founded 1601) and the University (founded 1532, though the building dates from 1750). The Monastery of San Martin Pinario, now a seminary, was founded in the 10th century and rebuilt in the 17th. The Monastery of San Francisco was supposedly founded by St. Francis of Assisi when he made a pilgrimage to Santiago in 1214. The Church of Santa Maria Salome and the collegiate church of Santa Marian la Real del Sar in the suburbs both date from the 12th century with later facades.

Santiago's chief economic activities apart from agriculture and the artistic industries of silverwork, jetwork, and wood engraving, include brewing and the distillation of spirits, foundaries and the manufacture of linen, paper, furniture, soap and matches. Pop. (1991 prelim.) 87,472.

The second visit the degree of the second chakra. A thing that Glen and Rosa felt they had in abundance. Their own thoughts and hopes and a spirit within. Cathedral of Notre Dame la Dalbade, Toulouse.

Toulouse, a medieval county of southern France from the 8th to the 13th century. The courtship can be dated from AD 778, when Charlemagne attempted to create bulwarks against the Muslims of Spain. The great dynasty, however, dates from 849 when Count Fredelon, a vassal of King Pepin II of Aquitaine, delivered Toulouse to Charles II the Bald of France, who thereupon confirmed him as count Dying in 852. Fredelon left a heritage including Rouerge (around Rodez) and the Pyrenea countships of Pallars and Ribagorza as well as the Toulousain to his brother Raymond I, who added Limousin to it; but Septimania was then probably detached.

Marriages and partitions changed the extent of the counts' dominion. By 1053 it included Quercy, the Albigeois (around Albi) and Rouergue. Raymond IV and his son Bertrand (died 1112) won the countship of Tripoli in the Holy Land; but at home the dynasty was weakened by quarrels with the House of Barcelona over Provence and with William IX of Aquitaine, who usurped the countship in 1098-100 and again in 1114-19. Towns such as Toulouse and vassals such as the Trencavel viscounts of Beziers and Carcassonne became practically autonomous. Raymond VII (died 1249) left the countship to his son-in-law Alphonse of Poitiers, on whose death in 1271 it was annexed to the French crown.

Toulouse, city, capital, Haute-Garonne department. Languedoc-Roussillon region of France, at the junction of the Canal Lateral a la Garonne and the Canal du Midi, where the Garonne River curves northwest from the Pyrenea foothills. Founded in ancient times, it was the stronghold of the Volcae Tectosages and developed as Tolosa during the Roman period. As capital of the Visigoths (AD 419-507) it was taken (508) by Clovis and included in the Merovingia kingdom. It successfully withstood a siege by Saracens in 721, was chief town of the Carolingian kingdom of Aquitaine, and after 778 because the seat of the feudal countship of Toulouse. Its counts adhered to the Cathari heresy and resisted the anti-heretic crusade in the 13th century. Afterward, many religious houses and the university (1229) were founded. Its Parlement established in 1420, had jurisdiction over Languedoc until the French Revolution. During the Wars of Religion in the 16th century, the city sided with the Catholic League Marshal Soult unsuccessfully fought the last batter of the Peninsular War against the Duke of Wellington outside the city on April 10, 1814.

The old city (vieux quartier) on the right high bank and surrounded by medieval fauboures (incorporated suburbs), embraces the business section. On the left low-lying bank is the faubourg of Saint-Cyprien. Toulouse, a bishopric (since the 4th century) and an archbishopric (since 1317), abounds its medieval churches—notably the Gothic cathedral of Saint-Etienne, the Romanesque basilica of Saint-Sernin, and the Gothic Eglise des Jacobins (mother church of the Dominican order and site of the tomb of St. Thomas Aquinas).

Many Renaissance and 16th-17th century buildings (built by prosperous woad (pastel) dye merchants) form one of the most splendid series in France and include the hotels de Bernuy, du Vieux Raisin, d-Espie and de Pierre. The Hotel d'Assezat houses the Academie des Jeux Floraux, founded in 1323 to encourage literary talent. The Duc de Montorency was executed (1632) in the interior courtyard of the Capitole (town hall).

Noteworthy art museums are those of Saint Raymond, des Augustins, and Paula Dupuy. The Ecole des Beaux Arts is on an 18th century riverside embankment and nearby, the Catholic Institute occupies a 16th century convent. The city's architecture was long characterized by rose-red brick. The most run down portions of the old centre have been demolished and replaced by an ultra-modern commercial centre, which clashes sharply with the older architecture. To make room for the vigorous population growth of the city, a new town, named Mirail (Miracle) was constructed to the southwest of the older neighbourhood of Saint-Cyprien.

Toulouse progressed commercially with the advent of railways in the 19th century. Diversified industrial development (which includes the manufacture of chemicals, aircraft and machinery) has been augmented by the availability of hydropower from the Pyrenees and natural gas from Lacq. The aerospace industry has seen extraordinary development research experiments, training of specialists, and production of vehicles (Caravelle, Concorde, Airbus, and military hardware). Because of its strategic position, with routes converging from north and south, it acts as a trading centre between the Mediterraean and the Aquitaine Basin, whose farm produce it markets. Pop (1982) 344,917.

The third level to gain virtue and honour in an unjust and misguided world. To cast out evil deeds and thoughts. To push forward for their dreams and demand courage through his or her own actions within the heart.

Sainte-Croix Cathedral in Orleans. Orleans being the capital of Loiret department and of the Centre region, north central France, south-southwest of Paris. The city stands on the banks of the Loire River in a fertile valley on the edge of the Beauce plain. Orleans, which derives its name from the Roman Aurelianum, was conquered by Julius Casear in 52 BC. It became an intellectual capital under Charlemagne, emperor from 800 to 814 ad in the 10th and 11th centuries it was the most important city in France after Paris. In 1429, during the Hundred Years' War (1337-1453), after it had been besieged for seven months by the English, the French national heroine St. Joan of Arc, the Maid of Orleans, and her troops delivered it. The victory continues to be celebrated annually (see Orleans, Siege of). Orleans was a Huguenot (Protestant) centre during the 16th century Wars of Religion, but the Roman Catholics took control of the city in 1572 after the Massacre of St. Bartholomew's Day, in which about 1,000 protestants were killed. It was occupied in 1870 by Prussians after a long siege. The city was severely bombed in World War II. Many buildings of historical and artistic interest were destroyed including the Jeanne-d'Arc Museum and the Church of St. Paul.

The Loire divides the town into two unequal parts. To the south lies the small Saint-Marceau quarter, a market gardening centre. The main part of the city stands on the northern bank of the Loire. The old quarter, surrounded by pleasant wide boulevards and quays along the river, was largely destroyed during World War II. It has been rebuilt in keeping with the style of the old 18th century town, with consideration for the imperatives of modern traffic. Beyond the boulevards new districts were built in the 1970s along the main roads leading out of the town.

Orleans is the centre of a modern road network; the railway junction just outside the city at Les Abrais is one of the most important in France. The university, founded in 1305, was abolished during the French Revolution, but the new one was established at la Source (source or springs of the Loire River) in 1962. Traditionally a centre for market gardening and horticulture (Orleans roses are famous), it has benefited from the decentralization of Paris, which took place after World War II and has developed new industries. These include textiles, food processing (nearly half of France's production of vinegar), and the manufacture of machinery (automobile accessories, agricultural equipment).

The Sainte-Croix Cathedral, begun in the 13th century, was largely destroyed by the Protestants in 1568. Henry IV, king of France from 1589 to 1610, gave funds for its reconstructions, and it was faithfully rebuilt (17th-19th century) in Gothic style. The 18th century towers were damaged in World War II but were later restored. The cathedral is about the same size as Notre-Dame of Paris. The stone and brick Renaissance Hotel de Ville (1549-55) was restored and enlarged in the 19th century. Pop. (1999) 112,833.

"The Fourth" love and compassion which Glen and Rosa, through their complete devotion and adoration, had passed this assessment with a natural love for life and humanity.

Chartres Cathedral, Chartres town, capital of Eure-et-Loir department. Centre region, northwestern France, southwest of Paris. The town is built on the left bank of the Eure River, ad the spires of its famous cathedral are a landmark on the plain of Beauce. Wide boulevards bordered by elms, encircle the told town with its deep narrow streets that lead down to picturesque houses by the river. The modern city has seen much recent growth in the neighbouring plain, which is an important route between Paris and the Loire Valley; and toward Brittany.

The main part of the great cathedral of Notre-Dame at Chartres was built in less than 30 years in the mid 13th century, when high Gothic architecture was at its purest. The cathedral was built to replace a 12th-century church of which only the crypt, the base of the towers, and the west façade remain. Remarkable 13th-century stained glass windows and a Renaissance choir screen add to the beauty of the edifice. Another notable church is Saint Pierre built mainly in the 13th century. A museum is housed on the former Episcopal Palace, dating from the 17th and 18th centuries.

Chartres, named after a Celtic tribe, the Carnutes, who made it their principal Druidic centre, was attacked several times by the Normans and was burned by them in 858. In the Middle Ages it became a countship and was held by the families of Blois and Champagne. The city was sold to the king of France in 1286, but during the Hundred Years' War (1337-1453), the English occupied it for 15 years. Francis I raised it to the rank of a duchy in 1528. During the Wars of Religion, the

Protestants attached it unsuccessfully. Henry IV was crowned there in 1594. During World War II, the town was severely damaged. Chartres is a market town for the region of Beauce (the granary of France) and has agricultural industries (fertilizers and farm equipment). Other industries include brewing, perfumes, the manufacture of car accessories and electronic equipment. The proximity of Paris has stimulated its economic development. Pop (1990) 39,595.

"The Fifth", Glen was army and had seen destruction and death and unruly societies and nations through his spirit he had suffered. He had spoken to the hierarchy and voiced his feelings and performed his duties. Rosa had travelled the world and been a spokeswoman for her peers. The realisation of conduct and consciousness.

Notre Dame de Paris, also called Notre-Dame Cathedral, cathedral church in Paris, France. It is the most famous of the Gothic cathedrals of the Middle Ages and is distinguished for its size, antiquity and architectural interest.

Notre-Dame lies at the eastern end of the Ile de la Cite and was built on the ruins of two earlier churches, which were themselves predated by a Gallo-Roman temple dedicated to Jupiter. The cathedral was initiated by Maurice de Sully, bishop of Paris, who about 1160 conceived the idea of converting into a single building on a larger scale, the ruins of the two earlier basilicas. The foundation stone was laid by Pope Alexander III in 1163, and the high altar was consecrated in 1189. The choir, the western façade, and the nave were completed by 1250, and porches, chapels and other embellishments were added over the next 100 years.

Notre Dame Cathedral consists of a choir and apse, a short transept, and a nave flanked by double aisles and square chapels. Its central spire was added during the restoration in the 19th century. The interior of the cathedral is 427 by 157 feet (130 by 4 m) in plan, and the roof is 115 feet (35 m) high. Two massive Early Gothic towers (1210-50) crown the western façade, which is divided into three stories and has its doors adorned with fine Early Gothic carvings and surmounted by a row of figures of Old Testament kings. The two towers are 223 feet (68 m) high; the spires with which they were to be crowned were never added. At the cathedral's east end, the apse has large clerestory windows (added 1235-70) and is supported by single arch flying buttresses of the more daring Rayonnant Gothic style, especially notable for their boldness and grace. The cathedral's three great rose windows alone retain their 13th century glass.

Notre-Dame cathedral suffered damage and deterioration through the centuries, and after the French Revolution it was rescued from possible destruction by Napoleon, who crowned himself emperor of the French in the cathedral in 1804. Notre-Dame underwent major restorations by the French architect E-E Viollet-le-Duc in the mid-19th century. The cathedral is the setting for Victor Hugo's historical novel Notre-Dame de Paris (1831).

"The sixth" the most difficult to realise within the heart and soul. The talent and dedication that Rosa had was beyond reproach. She was a woman of many faces and had a façade that shone and a caring that surpassed all trials and tribulations. Glen was smart with a business brain and a humbleness that actually was a power aspirant in the world of benevolence and philanthropy.

Amiens Cathedral, Amiens city, capital of Somme department. Picardie region, principal city and ancient capital of Picardy, northern France in the Sombre River Valley, north of Paris. Famed since the European Middle Ages are its textile industry and its great Gotic Cathedral of Notre-Dame, one of the finest in France. Known as Samarobriva in pre-Roman times and capital of the Ambiani (whence the modern name), Amiens became a Roman city, Christianized in the 4th century by St. Firmin, its first bishop. Its territory, became the medieval countship of Amienois, and its citizens profited from rivalry between bishop and count to gain a charter early in the 12th century. The peace of Amiens (1802) marked a short pause in the Napoleonic Wars. In 1914, after a brief incursion into the city, the invading Germans dug in 18 miles (29 km) east; their final drive in 1918 was stopped 8 miles (13 km) from the city. In World War II, Amiens was occupied by the Germans. After serious damage in both wars, the city centre was rebuilt.

The old part of Amiens, including the reconstructed 17th century city hall, the 15th century Church of Saint-Germain, and the ancient theatre with the Louis XVI façade, is latticed with seven branches of the river.

The cathedral was begun in 1220 on the plan of Robert de Luzarches and was finished about 50 years later (there were subsequent additions). Its galleried and rose-windowed façade, pierced by three portals and topped by twin towers, is splendid. It has a remarkable interior with a soaring nave and bold supporting columns, employing the logic of Romanesque while imposing the open and dramatic qualities of Gothic.

Apart from textiles, there is some manufacturing, including machinery, chemicals and tires. Truck farmers from the adjacent heavily watered bottom lands (hortillons) hold market in the city from small boats. Longeau, near Amiens, is an important railroad junction. Pop (1982) 130,302.

The seventh and most vital of the oracles (spiritual enlightenment).

Now they were back at Rosslyn. The crown chakra, the elite, the joining of the circle. The finality of the square. The fulfilment and consolidation of the "whole being". The comfort in knowing that you are one within the glory of utopian splendour.

The completion of the journey ceased in Scotland where Glen had his ancestral home. Glen's father was showing signs of illness. Doctors warned of pipe smoking and cigarette use and the diagnosis spelt out angina. Little time was left. Glen was saddened, Rosa distraught. There was a strong bond between son and father through the decades. A great tradition had been passed down into the close relationships of this Scottish family. Integrity, principles and reputations were vitally important. Glen being the only son would take on the mantle and name in every sense and reason.

It was a quiet funeral, private and solemn. Entured in his family crypt he lay in state for his mournful visitors.

Christmas had passed by almost unnoticed. But January 1st 1977, the date of his passing was an inauspicious time. They, Glen, Rosa and Glen's mother walked away for the last time after another visit. Glen in a black crombie overcoat, Rosa in a dark blue cashire full length double breasted cloak, like an overcoat that swirled around her feet and attractive short heeled red ankle high booties laced up at the sides. A red, white and blue tam-o-shanter sat upon her long strawberry blonde, gleaming hair. Glen's mum in a tartan short cape pelerine type over garment, and a tight knee length black rayon dress, white shoes and handbag. Rosa held a small red velvet purse with a gold plated clasp. They hugged and strolled side by side out of the graveyard of "God's acre".

THE KUNDALINI SERPENT
VULCAN
THE CHAKRAS
THE EIGHTH CHAKRA

THE KUNDALINI SERPENT

These short paragraphs gives one an in depth insight to the workings of "The Kundalini Serpent". The explanation herein is a little indefinite and obscure to a mere mortal. But then again I relate to the control and power of the "Human", to trust and consider their own ideology, conviction and principles in the search for understanding, knowledge and self belief.

The Kundalini Serpent

In my essay 'The Secret Knowledge of Nibiru' I described the possible connection between the Dark Star and the Eighth Sphere of the Theosophists (1). It seems that this Eighth Sphere was once a closely guarded secret of Madame Blavatsky's Theosophy school, itself an already rather esoteric discipline. However, the Theosophist A.P. Sinnett publically drew attention to a belief held by Inner Order esotericists about an invisible Sphere which was counter-balanced by the Moon (2). This revelation isn't exactly news, of course, as Sinnett's faux-pas was made at the end of the 19th Century. But it may have some relevance to my own research into possible ancient Dark Star symbols contained within esoteric lore.

On the face of it this piece of esoteric trivia doesn't exactly set the world alight. Until the significance of the counter-balancing of the Moon is considered. In Alchemy, Luna balances the Sun in a divine coupling that hints at the Yin/Yang relationship in Taoism, or the relationship between the Hindu Shakti and Shiva. What business does the 'Eighth Sphere' have counter-balancing the Moon when the task already clearly falls to Sol? This usurper runs the risk of over-turning one of the most basic tenets of accepted ancient wisdom; the duality at the heart of reality. The Duality would be in danger of becoming a Trinity of three celestial bodies. The Sun and Moon would have another contender vying for their pre-eminence. Is this why the existence of the 'Eighth Sphere' was once held as such an important secret by the esotericists of Theosophy?

Vulcan

What evidence is there that this Eighth Sphere relates to an undiscovered planet whose symbolic character rivals the Sun itself? Another strand of Planet X research involves the fabled 'Vulcan', the Roman god of fire. Barry Warmkessel's search for Vulcan is based to some extent upon the writings of Madame Blavatsky, from her work 'The Secret Doctrine'. According to Warmkessel, Blavatsky herself lays down the clues as to where to find the hidden planet, which she calls Vulcan (3).

Once again, clues to the existence of Planet X are to be found in esoteric writings. If Blavatsky bases her claims upon an ancient tradition that she is privy to then then we can conclude that the Dark Star was indeed the subject of a secret tradition, and may represent the Eighth Sphere that 'counter-balances' the Moon.

Given its Theosophical name of 'Vulcan', the concept that the Dark Star is a warm body such as a brown dwarf becomes more probable still. Not only that, but Vulcan is guarded by a 'bevy of monkeys (seven in all)', seemingly alluding to the fiery Dark Star's seven companions, or moons (2). The above detail is of Vulcan's Chariot from the 'Months' fresco in the Palazzo Schifanoia, Ferrara, as described by Mark Hedsel.

It would be certainly be difficult to explain the seven companions if Vulcan simply symbolised the Sun, and Vulcan does not appear to represent a constellation either. With the clue from the Theosophists about the Eighth Sphere we can begin to appreciate the subtleties of the esoteric message. Perhaps other esoteric paths can enlighten us further.

The Chakras

The Hindu or Tibetan system of Chakras describes the centres of energy within the human body that can be discovered and activated through meditation. Classically there are seven chakras, although there appear to be a myriad of other minor chakras dependent upon what you read. Bob Frissell contends that the chakras are like 'lenses through which we interpret reality' (4) with each chakra related to a level of human consciousness. Perhaps on a more mundane level this is related to Maslow's hierarchy of needs, but the act of self-knowledge through meditation is the key to the spiritual progress of the adept in Frissell's quasi-religious context. I'm no expert on Eastern

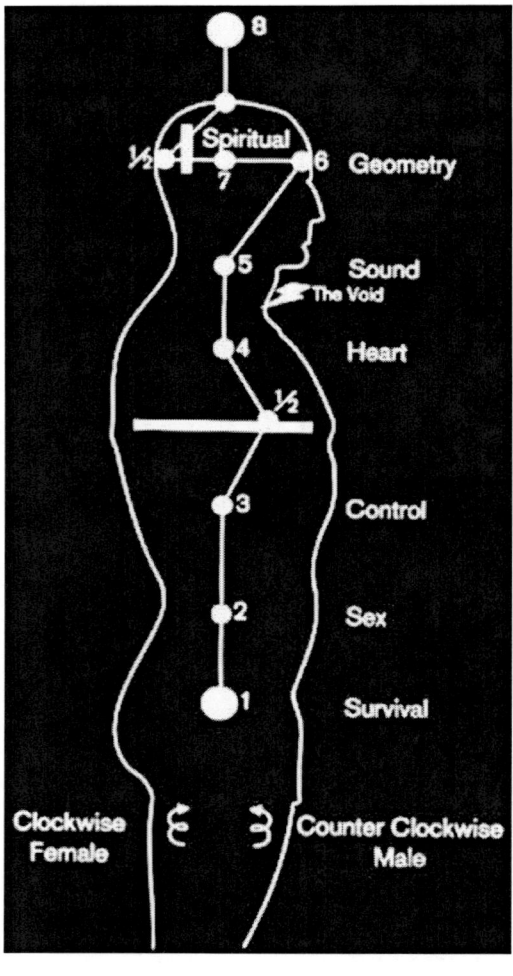

religion, but I think I'm correct in saying that the Theosophists were interested in amalgamating Eastern and Western philosophies, and drew extensively upon the religious ideas of the Indian sub-continent. As Peter Marshall explains in the context of the study of alchemy:

"The Theosophical Society, founded in New York in 1875 by Madame Helena P. Blavatsky, took up the seventeenth-century Rosicrucian programme of building a bridge between science and religion and of developing the latent spiritual powers of humanity. The Masters of Theosophy were said to guide

humanity's destiny from their headquarters in Tibet, the centre of Buddhist alchemy. The teachings of Ku–Hu–Mi, mentioned by the Rosicrucians, were made known to advanced Theosophists by Madame Blavatsky who claimed to have been one of his personal students in Tibet". (5)

So it wouldn't be a big stretch to infer that the Theosophists were influenced by the same ancient teachings from which were derived knowledge of the chakras. In other words, the Eighth Sphere has a place in the Microcosm as well as the Macrocosm. This would be in keeping with the alchemical tenet of Hermes Trismegistus:

"That which is above is like that which is below, and that which is below is like that to which is above, to accomplish the miracles of the one thing". (6)

Marshall draws our attention to the pranas, or primary channels of energies of the Nadi tree. The 5 pranas are similar to the 7 chakras, and are associated with colours, planets and elements (the latter explaining the number 5, no doubt). The 7 ancient planets are partially doubled up to fit into the prana system, which seems somewhat contrived. For instance, both Venus and the Moon are represented by the Apana channel, while Mars and the Sun find a common home in the Samana channel (5). The seven planets would seem to fit better within the Chakra system, and such a correspondence is alluded to by Rachel Finney who recently pointed out to me the relationship between the chakras, planets and various esoteric centres in Europe:

"Each of the major cathedrals along the pilgrimage were on ancient sites representing the seven major chakras of Europe. 'Pilgrims' or 'initiates' went to each one in turn to learn the 'knowledge' associated with each chakra. This actually goes back to the time of the Druids. When I say went to each one in turn, that might mean several years of study at each one in order to master the widsom and insights for that level/degree of study.

The sites were:

Cathedral of St. James at Compostela	(Moon Oracle)	—base chakra
Notre-Dame de Dalbade Tolouse	(Mercury Oracle)	—sacral chakra
Orleans Cathedral	(Venus Oracle)	—solar pelxus chakra
Chartres Cathedral	(Sun Oracle)	—heart chakra
Notre Dame de Paris	(Mars Oracle)	—throat chakra
Amiens Cathedral	(Jupiter Oracle)	—brow chakra
Rosslyn Chapel	(Saturn Oracle)	—crown chakra"

(7,10)

The upwards motion through the chakras corresponds with the movement through the celestial spheres as they were understood in ancient times, so one would expect that a hidden, eighth ancient planet would be represented by an eighth chakra located above the head. Also, one could reasonably anticipate that an eighth geographical centre of esoteric learning, of more significance even than the famous Rosslyn Chapel, would exist for the most learned Initiates of European esoteric mysteries. In keeping with the secrecy of the Eighth Sphere, this centre would also remain hidden and jealously guarded.

The Eighth Chakra

So is there an eighth chakra? I quick look at the diagram above, from Frissell's book, shows that there is a belief in an eighth chakra located above the head. A search through various Internet sites devoted to this kind of religious study confirmed his opinion. So, the eighth chakra appears to be associated closely with the normally dormant energy that itself travels up through the other chakra centres. This is known as the Kundalini and, significantly, this energy is associated with a spiralling, or circulating, fire serpent (8). Here's Peter Marshall again with some words of warning:

"I was told by the tantrist Swami Yogi Prakash that awakening the sleeping power of Kundalini is not to be taken lightly. It requires careful initiation and long practice. To raise its energy is literally playing with the fire of the cosmos". (5)

I am greatly encouraged by this association between the 'serpent fire energy' of Kundalini, that lies dormant before its potentially catastrophic journey through the known chakras, and the hidden Dark Star whose perihelion passage could be equally devastating through the system. 'As above, so below', as the alchemists say.

I am very tempted to propose that the Dark Star is the ancient source of the symbol of the Eighth Sphere, itself incorporated into the religious teachings of the Hindu and Buddhist yogis in the form of the eighth heavenly chakra. I think that the Dark Star is the third apex of the celestial Trinity (9), and is beautifully alluded to in this verse from the Hevajra Tantra:

"There are Moon and Sun, and between them the Seed. This last is that Being, whose nature is Joy Supreme" (5)

In the alchemical diagrams of Renaissance Europe, the third aspect of the Trinity is often expressed as a bird, either the 'Hermes bird' or the fiery Phoenix. It encroaches upon the duality of the Sun and Moon and is sometimes symbolised by Mercury.

The alchemical dragon Azoth, for instance, is shown with three celestial heads, the Moon, the Sun and a third 'sun', depicted as mercury symbolically, yet like Sol in radiance and power. I believe that this is the "Philosopher's Mercury", rather than plain-old Mercury, and is the secret ingredient alluded to in the instructions for making the Red Elixir, or Philosopher's Stone.

Is this 'Philosopher's Mercury' symbolised by the Eighth Sphere, or planet? Indeed, does the red Stone itself, that is said to be simultaneously seen, yet unseen, reflect the nature of the Dark Star? I suspect that this may be a closely guarded secret of alchemy, although their knowledge of this eighth body may be understood in an altogether different way by esotericists. Nevertheless, the hidden physical and celestial source of the symbolism is one and the same.

Furthermore, the relationship between the cross and the number eight is hinted at by the English alchemist John Dee in his *Monas Hieroglyphica.* Discussing a glyph formed by the symbol of Mercury in Aries, Marshall points out this possible high secret:

'Dee hints darkly that the cross in a 'most secret manner' signifies the 'octonary' which earlier magi did not understand but which the initiated reader 'will especially note'. I mention this for the adpts among you'. (6)

So does this tie the Eighth Sphere in with the Messianic Star, amalgamating East and West as the Theosophists endeavour to show us? Was the original Christian concept of the Trinity a bringing forth of Hermetic hidden knowledge about the importance of the Phoenix? All of this speculative reasoning brought me a moment of self-reflection, one that may be shared by others interested in the search for Planet X, the Dark Star or Nibiru.

I wonder whether our Macrocosmic search for this hidden fiery 'planet' represent our own spiritual yearning to achieve self-enlightenment through the release of inner Kundalini energy? In other words, deep down the hunt for the Eighth celestial sphere, or planet, is a spiritual journey as much as an empirical one. Being of Western stock, and raised on English empirical philosophy, I cannot claim to have a full grasp of the deep meanings attached to the Eastern teachings regarding the chakras. But the alchemical associations are compelling, and an underlying pattern has emerged that brings a simple solution to the mystery of the Theosophist's Eighth Sphere. That fiery realm of heaven may exist within, as well as without.

As for my extrapolation of a hidden centre of esoteric learning; that question remains unanswered in my mind. If such a place exists, I would expect it to be a major focus of Freemasonry and other Western esoteric schools, and would be represented by the serpent fire in its symbolism. Perhaps a link can be made here with 'Chnoubis', the lion-headed cosmic serpent of Gnostic traditions.

Perhaps this eighth geographical chakra is lost in the same way as the Dark Star itself, an ancient place long forgotten in time and place. If we follow the logic of the European centres of esoteric learning, then they follow a trail northward to Rosslyn chapel in Scotland.

The location of the eighth chakra is above the head in a bodily sense, while beyond the family of planets in an astronomical sense (the Dark Star hidden among the comets), so would be north of Scotland geographically. Which potentially takes us into all-new territory . . .

Written by <u>Andy Lloyd</u>, author of '<u>The Dark Star</u>' (2005), '<u>Ezekiel One</u>' (2009) and '<u>The Followers of Horus</u>' (2010) © 10th September 2002

ROSSLYN CHAPEL

Rosslyn Chapel, properly named the **Collegiate Chapel of St Matthew,** was founded on a small hill above Roslin Glen as a Catholic collegiate church (with between four and six ordained canons and two boy choristers) in the mid-15th century. Rosslyn Chapel and the nearby Roslin Castle are located at the village of Roslin, Midlothian, Scotland.

The chapel was founded by William Sinclair, 1st Earl of Caithness (also spelled "Sainteclaire/Saintclair/Sinclair/St. Clair") of the Sinclair family, a noble family descended in part from Norman knights from the commune of Saint-Clair-sur-Epte in northern France, using the standard designs the medieval architects made available to him. Rosslyn Chapel is the third Sinclair place of worship at Roslin—the first being in Roslin Castle and the second (whose crumbling buttresses can still be seen today) in what is now Roslin Cemetery.

The purpose of the college was to celebrate the Divine Office throughout the day and night and also to celebrate Holy Mass for all the faithful departed, including the deceased members of the Sinclair family. During this period the rich heritage of plainsong (a single melodic line) or polyphony (vocal harmony) would be used to enrich the singing of the liturgy. An endowment was made that would pay for the upkeep of the priests and choristers in perpetuity and they also had parochial responsibilities.

After the Scottish Reformation (1560) Roman Catholic worship in the chapel was brought to an end, although the Sinclair family continued to be Roman Catholics until the early 18th century. From that time the chapel was closed to public worship until 1861 when it was opened again as a place of worship according to the rites of the Scottish Episcopal Church.

In later years the chapel has featured in speculative theories regarding Freemasonry and the Knights Templar.

Architecture

The original plans for Rosslyn have never been found or recorded, so it is open to speculation whether or not the chapel was intended to be built in its current layout. Its architecture is considered to be some of the finest in Scotland.

Construction of the chapel began on 20 September 1456, although it has often been recorded as 1446. The confusion over the building date comes from the chapel's receiving its founding charter to build a collegiate chapel in 1446 from Rome. Sinclair did not start to build the chapel until he had built houses for his craftsmen. Although the original building was to be cruciform in shape, it was never completed; only the choir was constructed, with the retro-chapel, otherwise called the Lady chapel, built on the much earlier crypt (Lower Chapel) believed to form part of an earlier castle. The foundations of the unbuilt nave and transepts stretching to a distance of 90 feet were recorded in the 19th century. The decorative carving was executed over a forty-year period. After the founder's death, construction of the planned nave and transepts was abandoned—either from lack of funds, lack of interest or a change in liturgical fashion. The Lower Chapel (also known as the crypt or sacristy) should not be confused with the burial vaults that lie underneath Rosslyn Chapel.

The chapel stands on fourteen pillars, which form an arcade of twelve pointed arches on three sides of the nave. At the east end, a fourteenth pillar between the penultimate pair form a three-pillared division between the nave and the Lady chapel. The three pillars at the east end of the chapel are named, from north to south: the Master Pillar, the Journeyman Pillar, and most famously, the Apprentice Pillar. These names for the pillars date from the late Georgian period — prior to this period they were called The Earl's Pillar, The Shekinah and the Prince's pillar.

'Musical' boxes

Among Rosslyn's many intricate carvings are a sequence of 213 cubes or boxes protruding from pillars and arches with a selection of patterns on them. It is unknown whether these patterns have any particular meaning attached to them—many people have attempted to find information coded into them, but no interpretation has yet proven conclusive.

One recent attempt to make sense of the boxes has been to interpret them as a musical score. The motifs on the boxes somewhat resemble geometric patterns seen in the study of cymatics. The patterns are formed by placing powder upon a flat surface and vibrating the surface at different frequencies. By matching these Chladni patterns with musical notes corresponding to the same frequencies, the father-and-son team of Thomas and Stuart Mitchell produced a tune which Stuart calls the *Rosslyn Motet*, if this can be played, and if this sound can vibrate Enough inside Rosslyn, it will unlock a long lost secret hidden in the masonry.

So in effect "music" is the key. From the first birds to the ancients, music has been the life and soul of the universe. The cosmos actually sings. Music through the ages, has transformed the human element and calmed the very beast of natural progression. If music can make patterns then it can move emotions. Re-animating the living breathing dynamics of creation. The mathematics of sound and music is the core of divinity. Music heals, soothes and pleases.

Take the pathfinders, the creationists from Mozart to Beethoven, Brahms, List, Strauss, great singers of their generation. Bands, operatics, church choirs, gregorian monks with their dedication. The Beatles, the Rolling Stones, Abba, Al Martino, Frank Sinatra, Perry

Como (all the greats). "Elvis" actually was brought up in the heart of religion "Memphis". Memphis was the name of a ruined city in Egypt, the ancient centre of lower Egypt on the Nile. Administrative and artistic centre, sacred to the worship of "Ptah" (Egyptian myth). Ptah was the deification of the primordial mound in the ennead in (cosmonogy) which is the study of the origin and development of the universe, such as the solar system. Memphis was a source of universal power and reverence. "Elvis" means to god most high, in America. Elvites or Elvis is now a veneration of worship. El is God, Vis means strength and power. [Music] through the decades, it's a monumental thing that moves people of all ages. That's why hysteria erupts. Music is inspirational or emotionally uplifting. Music creates a pattern so music moves the soul, the internal spirit. Tony had the gift, the gift to sing and create. His music is sublime and has creative power to transform humanity to sublime realization, or so he would like to think.

It was quiet the year from October to October. The recession had taken its toll. Things were a little somber around the area of Merseyside and the Wirral. Everything seemed to be on a knife edge. Even the music scene had given away to a soba influence, the spark had somehow diminished. There was a heaviness that filled the atmosphere, a dullness persisted.

The youth was out of control, gang warfare, gun crimes. The internet i.e. a sexual exploitation, child cruelty molestations, wars, terrorism, violent earthquakes, floods. The most peaceful of communities ravaged by violence and political upheaval.

The years that had passed were unblessed and catastrophic. But every cloud has a silver lining, the darkest hour is always before dawn.

There's a light at the end of the tunnel. Considering these disasters, atrocities, dilemmas, natural phenomena, is there on balance a fulcrum that supports, that sustains, that represents the coming of an age when the world will exist in a sublime utopia, or does that only correspond to the mind and thoughts of an individual.

22ⁿᵈ October 2010.

The winter had settled itself on Britain. The dark days were upon the land. This was the time the family would head off for their autumn break.

Spain was still hot enough and the sun would still give one a nice even tan. The long weekend was a welcome change from their workaday environment. It was Glen and Rosa's favourite destination. Lamata in Alicante was their special retreat.

The apartment overlooked the glorious soft sandy beach. With the esplanade below the veranda, they could view the Mediterranean and watch the hoards of sun seekers amble along past café bars and restaurants. The pristine neatly paved sidewalk decorated with borders of shrubs and plants. The warm waters lapping the shore. Children and holiday makers basking in the baking sun, skipping playfully with beach balls, paddling with their friends and parents. Teenagers playing head tennis, topless beauties splashing in the ocean, families under parasols picnicking, oiling themselves with suntan lotion, a wonderful spectacle of life buoyant with happiness freedom and ease. People relaxed with drinks and food in the café bars. Pizzas, paella, steaks, "Tortilla de Patatas", Glen, Rosa and Luke's favourite snack.

The apartment had all the mod cons. Luke was always happy to be asked along by his parents. He always looked forward to it at this time of year usually October 23ʳᵈ. He would have his game-boys, computer console, pool table and Jacuzzi. He had all he needed to keep himself occupied. It held three bedrooms with air conditioning, a ground and a first floor with black marble floors and walls. The ground floor stretched into an open kitchen area, very adequate for their needs. They ate out most days. A massive plasma screen TV was perched on a wall between two large Tuscan style columns. A massive deep cushioned burgundy coloured settee sat upon a flower embossed dark rich axminster carpet. A solid highly polished oak coffee table rested centre stage, palm trees sprang from brass pots in every corner. It was a haven, a veritable paradise.

Tony would stay a couple of days at the halls of residence. Parties were a must, and Tony was a welcome participant. His music (guitar playing) (singing) was a special part of proceedings. He was a potential rock star and the congregation were awe-inspired. A hero amid the muses and his musical contemporaries.

He arrived back at Rosslyn on the 25th October. He settled in at his home and reveled in its homeliness and distinctly welcoming aura. It was 26th October at 10 p. m. Tony was resting sleepy eyed when the clatter of feet and gentle close of the main door broke his peaceful slumber. "Tony, Tony, Tony!!" cried Luke, suitcases clumped to the floor in the hall. His family arrived home from their stay in Spain. Luke rushed in to greet his loving brother with a rollicking high five and a massive hug. He greeted his father with a hand shake and a gracious smile and his mother with the most sweetest kiss to the cheek and warm hands clasped around her shoulders. They talked, laughed and filled in any areas they had missed while away. With gossip information they sipped tea and brushed up on health, school, university, work and the time in Spain.

"You look great mum!" Tony pronounced "And dad you look so healthy!" Tony exclaimed, proud and concerned that they had arrived home safe and sound. "Meet any nice young senoritas?" said Tony. Again, looking at Luke with cow eyes. Luke would gesture tight lipped and narrow his eyes towards Tony. Looking meaningfully embarrassed but with a shadow of a smile on his face, they dispersed and retired to their beds.

27th October 2010.

The family raised themselves a little late the next day. Tony was catching up on sleep after some late night partying. Luke, Glen and Rosa after their commuting and plane flight. But still it was 10 a.m. They were not the type for lying in after noon in the day. There was a light breakfast of croissants, orange juice and coffee. Luke had secured a day paint-balling. "Oh no dear, you be careful!" Rosa exclaimed as she was clearing the table. "It's just paint mum, it washes off easily and we wear protective clothing!" replied Luke. He left the dining room and skipped out of the house and down the path. Meeting friends at the gate after he was buzzed on his mobile phone. He always had it on "vibrate" around the house. Respect and courtesy was a big thing in Luke's life.

Glen was now in the study going through some unread letters. Tony was reading in his room. Autobiographies were his favourite, usually profiles of rock stars and film stars, but his material could be profound and varied.

On an adjacent wall embossed with deep yellow wallpaper were five prints; Mohammed Ali, Bruce Lee, Frank Sinatra, Humphrey Bogart and the famous photo of the Beatles crossing Abbey Road. These people were his idols, his inspiration. In a gold encrusted frame (the portrait of Shakespeare) writing on parchment with his quill, adorned his antique desk. He was a might star struck and starry eyed at times. He was still a young man and fed on the stimulation of his heroes, past and present. It was important for him to assimilate the way things were materializing, he may, in fact become a member of that exalted circle in a very prodigious manner.

Rosa busied herself most times, cleaning, cooking, arranging furniture and the flowers, tending the garden on occasion.

Gerta did not appear at holiday time but could be drafted in as soon as school and work days began again. There was a gardener once a week, he was hardly ever seen and kept things flourishing in winter and full bloom in Spring and Summer. Ted was an able fifty five year old semi retired. He had traveled the world and had landscaped gardens in the most far off reaches of the planet. Some stories he told were a bit outrageous and embellished. But he was true to his work. He could be seen riding his bike around the village of Seacombe waving at people smiling happily.

That evening Tony, Luke, Rosa and Glen were seated together in the lounge after dinner, chatting in general. There had been some odd occurrences and Luke wanted to talk about it.

"The doves have been a little strange lately. Different, scared of my touch, off their food, reluctant to take their exercise, afraid to leave the loft. I've never known them that way. Can't work it out, and I'm getting shivers down my spine and a sensation like ice running over my skin. I can't sleep for the worry of it all," said Luke. Rosa covered the back of his hand with her own.

"It'll be OK sweetheart," she replied, patting his hand as he squeezed nearer to her on the large leather Chesterfield.

"You know", Rosa spoke. I've been feeling something pulling at my hair especially at night, waking me from my sleep. Very weird."

Glen chipped in, "I get a distinct smell. Not the best, I must add. I know Gerta keeps things immaculately clean and tidy. And, of course, as you do also my dear Rosa. Rosa looked down and nodded, in a bow.

"Thank you Glen," she said in gratitude, looking back to the boys with a contented smile. Tony sat pensive and studied his family. Lips closed in a pout, sullen and thoughtful. Never had he felt any presence, or sensations of the macabre. Never had he been in fear of such things. Never had he succumbed to the irrational hysterics of the supernatural. It was hard to accept the facts or asperses that had moulded themselves into the hearts and minds of people throughout history. But he was anxious and concerned about such happenings, especially within his own family. A family he truly adored beyond all measure. This was not what he wanted to hear. Bad omens, unnatural events did not happen in this family, and it was a shock that sent slight tremors though his relaxed but fraught and over-charged body.

There are stories surrounding Rosslyn and the shore line at Seacombe. Ghost ships, apparitions, appearing and disappearing. Characters in odd dress. Roguish seafaring men silhouetted in the light of a bonfire, on the sands of the Mersey. Distant cries of men splashing in the waters calling for help. Creaking boughs, the groaning of timbers under the strain of a floundering vestle. Hearsay, drunken revellers imagination. Folk tales? Funny thing about the supernatural we never get to the bottom of it. Undiscovered elements that pervade the natural world. Mysteries that persist in all walks of life. The crux of the matter is that the human race has been saturated with the phenomena throughout the ages, in the media, in folk law, and relative gossip. If ever the truth should come out in a factual state then the world is not going to be overwhelmed by fear or surprise. Conditioning the word "conditioning" sounds a little suspect especially considering the U.F.O prodigy. The over powering sense that the universe is teaming with life. Other worlds, realms far beyond our imagination. Glimpses of these wordly phenomena is vast in all areas of the planet. Later that evening Tony had his arm looped over Luke's shoulders as they climbed the stairway to their rooms. "OK mate!" Tony enquired in a concerned brotherly way. Luke stayed silent and thoughtful, his head slightly bowed. They reached the open landing at the top of the stairs.

"Is there really an evil spirit, Tony," asked Luke.

"There's bad elements in life, Luke," Tony replied. "The make-up of the universe, force of nature good and bad. Hurricanes, storms, tornado's. Places in the earth's atmosphere where there is no let up, no peace or tranquillity. Only a hellish existence presides. Maybe there's people, things, beasts, the un-dead. The wicked, the evil downcasts of God's judgement. The undisputed facts of physics, other realms. Hidden depths of the world's make-up that we don't know about. If you look at life itself, it's like that. The poor, the needy, the tortured, the unfortunate, the unlucky, ones who suffer, volcano's, tsunamis, earthquakes. Horrors that exist before our very eyes. Who knows if there's worse to come, or some unforeseen terrors that have not revealed themselves. Live your life Luke, but be on your guard for destructive patterns that may corrupt or bend reality. Be yourself. Do not judge, then you will not be judged. Keep your heart pure as possible. But be happy, live your life. But do not step over into sin and depravity."

"Study well Luke, get that degree son! Don't let anything get in the way, you're a great lad, you've got a lovely personality, you care about people, you haven't got a violent bone in your body. You love your birds. The world needs someone like you. I only wish you the best kiddo! If you need me Luke I'm just down the hall". Tony stroked the side of Luke's face and fluffed his hair, gently. "Stay cool my mate, see you in the mornin!". They parted. As Luke entered his room Tony made a double clicking sound from the corner of his mouth. Luke looked up. Tony winked and raised his thumb with an assuring smile. They slept well that night.

28th October 2010

This was Thursday. Tony was at his Ju-Jitsu headquarters training hard for his second dan. A prestigious certificate in top flight martial arts. Luke was exercising his precious birds.

Glen and Rosa were preparing themselves for dinner at a top class restaurant in the town. Glen took all of an hour to prepare for the evening out, Rosa a little longer, a half hour longer. Glen would wait in the study and pour himself a large martini dry with a dash of lemonade and a cube of ice. His "aperitif". He would never be seen the worse for wear but, he did get tipsy on occasions.

Tony arrived home. It was 7.30 p.m. Luke would never be left alone in the house unless it was a very rare occurrence. A taxi arrived at the gates, Rosa and Glen headed off for the night, Glen in his beige suit and silk tie, white shirt and his brogues on his feet, helped Rosa into the back of the cab. White stilettos graced her defined well crafted ankles. Her bolero styled jacket and sleek trouser leggings gave her the look of a Spanish matador. She could still wow a crowd with her dress sense. The pale blue trouser suit embellished the white strapped handbag and frilly blouse. Elegance personified. Tony and Luke decided on an early night. When Rosa and Glen returned, it was a night of unbridled passion that ended proceedings.

29th October 2010

After breakfast at 9 a.m. (8 a.m. work days) give or take a minute here or there. The family, except Luke who would race off to the Dovecot to comfort his doves refresh their food and drink and let them out for some exercise. Would read the selection of morning papers, delivered every morning at 8.30 a.m. The Telegraph, The Times, The Independent and The Daily Mail and Express. The Wirral Champion magazine was always somewhere around. They would sit peaceful perusing the tabloids and broadsheets. Coffee was always fresh and hot on the percolator ring. Groceries were dropped off three times a week by the grocer himself. He was a friend of "The Barringtons of Seacombe" as he would always refer to them. The butcher too would visit with fresh meat. Steaks, chicken, mince meat. "12 p.m." Glen returned to the study. Rosa departed for the annexe to finish some delicate needle work. Tony was now showering after a strenuous work out in his room. He would go bowling with Annette today. Something he had never done with a girl friend or lover. Annette would whisper in his ear at times, guiding him, suggesting things, re-routing his thought taking him to different levels of social activities. They would dine out, see a movie, go to the races. Chester Racecourse was a fabulous day out in the summer months and only minutes away in the car. Tony owned a Mercedes sports. Dark blue with a fabulous sound system—C/D front loader. Sun roof and leather interior. He commuted on most days and would only drive on certain occasions. He looked after his prized possessions. It was dinner and another restful night for the family.

30ᵗʰ October 2010, Saturday.

The family stayed home this day. They would not risk driving or venturing out especially late in the evening. Mischief night and shenanigans were abroad. A quiet uneventful twenty four hours was the order of the day. Rosa watered the flowers, Glen was e-mailing in the study. Luke would watch a selection of movies from his well stocked video library. This would be for hours and then there was the discovery channel, his favourite. This boy was well educated and fulfilled. He absorbed information on a grand scale. Tony was reading in his room. Robert Burns; A Life by Ian McIntyre was the book in question. It was an insight to Burns himself and his existence and times from 1759 in Scotland. A really tough read but Tony persevered and finished after a period of weeks. He also trawled through the book; A life of William Shakespeare by Sidney Lee. Two accomplishments he was proud of.

Luke and Tony were a little past dressing up and wearing masks.

A lantern style pumpkin hung in place of a flower bowl in the porch. This was as much as Rosa could accept in the circumstances. As far as she was concerned there was enough of the macabre in the world. There were no small children to accommodate, no parties to attend, no gatherings of the clan, no midnight orgies of drink or drugs. As much as it was quaint and fun loving things were kept at a sober level. If anyone buzzed at the gates, children trick or treating, they would be offered confectionery, a tub of sweets, even money if Rosa felt so obliging. Tony would accompany his mother to the entrance of the home and the congregation would be pacified.

Christmas was more Rosa's style. Sometimes church was attended. Rosa and Glen gladly partook of sermons and services on Sunday mornings when the devoutness shone through.

Christmas time was glorious at Rosslyn. The massive tree in the hall. The lights and decorations luminous like a heavenly chapel in itself. The presents lovingly wrapped with affection. Fairy lights glowing around the façade, illuminating half of the Estate. The Christmas dinner, all of seven courses, with mince pies and coffee and liquors in the study and champagne to toast. This feast could take up to three hours to consume and enjoy, with laughter, fun chat and merriment the complete occasion for a family so much in unison with life, living and compassion.

A candelabra graced the centre of the festive table, brightly shining with twelve deep red candles.

Glen in his black tuxedo and crisp white dress shirt and bow tie. The boys in shiny blue mohair suits with black velvet collars highly polished black leather chelsea boots, black ties and white button down silk shirts.

Rosa looked like Christmas itself in her downy crimson coloured sequined dress that flowed like a soft ocean around her glittering countenance. Like a vision, her hair dancing in curls and swirls around her neck and shoulders, multicoloured ribbons hanging loosely here and there complimenting the flawless golden strands. Those lips so full and the colour of burgundy would enhance the marble features and delicate nuance of perfection. A true goddess.

THE BARRINGTON CHRISTMAS DINNER

MENU

Prawn Cocktail   or   Pate
Brown Bread   Toasted Fingers
Butter

. . . .

Consommé

(Beef soup with hot crispy rolls)

. . . .

Sole Mornay

(Fish and Cheese sauce)

. . . .

Sorbet (Mint)
Roast Turkey with trimmings (Cranberry Jelly), Roast Loin of Pork (Apple Sauce)

. . . .

Christmas Pudding   or   Chocolate Gateaux
with brandy sauce   with clotted cream

. . . .

Cheese Board
(Assorted cheese and biscuits).

. . . .

Petit Fours

. . . .

Coffee
Red/white/rose wine and vintage port

HALLOWEEN

One of the aspects of human nature is to gain balance in the face of fear and abandonment. To create a world within a world. Substantial laws, proclamations, codes are established rules deliberations. The conduct of life through history contains spirit energy and culture needed for a fine tuned universe. Natural processes formed within societies, folklore, superstition, juju, beliefs that prompt action. Halloween is one of these measures to inaugurate some sanity in a mysterious, surreptitious cosmos.

Our ancestors celebrated New Year on November 1st. They celebrated their New Year's Eve on October 31st.

Samhain (pronounced 'sow-in') marked the end of the "season of the sun" (summer) and the beginning of "the season of darkness and cold" (winter).

The Facts

Neither the word Halloween or the date 31st October are mentioned in any Anglo-Saxon text indicating that it was just an ordinary day a thousand years ago.

From the Medieval period (1066-1485) through to the 19th century, there is no evidence that 31 October was anything else other than the eve of All Saints day.

From the 19th century to the present day, 31st October has increasingly acquired a reputation as a night on which ghost, witches, and fairies, are especially active.

All Saints Day—1ˢᵗ November

In the year 835 AD the Roman Catholic church made 1ˢᵗ November a church holiday to honour all the saints. Although it was a joyous holiday it was also the eve of All Souls day, so in medieval times it became customary to pray for the dead on this date. Another name for All Saints day is 'All Hallows' (hallow is an archaic English word for 'saint'). The festival began on All Hallows Eve, the last night of October.

Where does the name Halloween originate from?

Halloween comes from All Hallow Even, the eve (night before) All Hallows day. Therefore, Halloween is the eve of All Saints day.

Evil spirits

The Celts believed that evil spirits came with the long hours of winter darkness. They believed that on that night the barriers between our world and the spirit world were at their weakest and therefore spirits were most likely to be seen on earth.

Bonfires

The Celts built bonfires to frighten the spirits away, and feasted and danced around the fires. The fires brought comfort to the souls in purgatory and people prayed for them as they held burning straw up high. Purgatory is a place where souls are temporarily punished for venial sins. After they have been punished enough, they are permitted to move on to heaven.

The fires of Halloween burned the strongest in Scotland and Ireland, where Celtic influence was most pronounced, although they lingered on in some of the northern counties of England until the early years of the last century.

Bonfire celebrations moved to 5th November

In England, the day of fires became 5th November (Bonfire Night), the anniversary of the Gunpowder plot of 1605, but its closeness to Halloween is more than a coincidence. Halloween and Bonfire Night have a common origin they both originated from pagan times, when the evil spirits of darkness had to be driven away with noise and fire.

Halloween Customs

In Lancashire, 'Lating' or 'Lighting the witches' was an important Halloween custom. People would carry candles from eleven to midnight. If the candles burned steadily the carriers were safe for the season, but if the witches blew them out, the omen was bad indeed.

In parts of the north of England Halloween was known as Nut-crack Night. Nuts were put on the fire and, according to their behaviour in the flames, forecast faithfulness in sweethearts and the success or failure of marriages.

Halloween was also sometimes called Snap Apple Night, in England. A game called snap apple was played where apples were suspended on a long piece of string. Contestants had to try and bite the apple without using their hands. A variation of the game was to fix an apple and a lighted candle at opposite end of a stick suspended horizontally and to swing the stick round. The object was to catch the apple between the teeth whilst avoiding the candle.

Many places in England combined Halloween with Mischief Night (celebrated on 4th November), when boys played all kinds of practical jokes on their neighbours. They changed shop signs, took gates of their hinges, whitewashed doors, and tied door latches.

Another tradition form which Halloween customs might have come from is a ninth century European custom, souling. It was a Christian festival where people would make house calls begging for soul cakes. it was believed that even strangers could help a soul's journey to heaven by saying prayers, so, in exchange for a cake they promised to pray for the donor's deceased relatives.

ow if Halloween is such an auspicious event and the veil between two worlds, (in fact, any world), is at its most transparent or superficial, then there can be elements of evil that persist in those realms. The devil may care to intervene and discredit, disrupt and destroy any incongruous efforts by the populous to proliferate. In fact, though scary and chilling in its light-hearted way it's a blessing, a human benevolence that transmits love and caring for the souls and forgotten spirits that once roamed the planet in their earthly state. It's for the connection of blood brothers and loved ones on their journey to the distant and forgotten lands to help and assist in their struggle to aspire to better levels. Its unique and true vocation is in fact awe-inspiring, even Godly. This is the time when the horror and devastation rained down on the Barrington household.

I t was the 31ˢᵗ October 2010 nearing the witching hour.

The mist descended like a cloak covering the land in a great shroud. Traffic slowed to a crawl. People felt their way through the streets of the town. Midnight was just but an hour away and light rain filled the cold air. Part of the incline that the Rosslyn mansion sat upon was completely engulfed in a thick, dense fog. It seemed to have a life of its own, creeping, enveloping everything in its path. Swirling ominously through the trees like a death knell. If one looked carefully, you could make out faces, apparitions, ghostly figures, glimpses of horrendous features. Evil specters like form fading in and out of the murky smog, staring, threatening, taunting.

Voices reverberated through the mist.

"Where are we?" Agga asked. "Rosslyn," said Melchin. Their voices pitchy high in a whispered tone.

Melchin spoke again, "The master said this was his next crusade, wiped from the face of the earth were his words! Yeh! and I've got to do his dirty work," Agga replied.

"Well you enjoy it sometimes, don't you!" answered Melchin.

"Mmm! We don't have much choice trapped in this body", added Agga. "Got to do his bidding until we can rise to another level!

"Shut up!" growled Melchin. "The boy's awake, he's reading, his window is open!" "Foolish boy! What's his name," uttered Agga.

"Luke!" answered Melchin.

"Oh that's a name from the Bible!"

"Shut up!" said Melchin again. "Look there's the dovecote with those lovely birds of his."

The dovecote was a beautiful thing in itself. A monument to peace and tranquillity, an effigy to all things sacred in the world. It was picturesque with its conical towers. It was painted white and was not unlike a castle with two domed turrets either sides of its main entrance and doorway, open steps with conifer trees in the two large Roman-style pots graced the frontage, where lush green lawns like billiard tables stood out in a magnificent green blaze. A white picket fence skirted the perimeter. A lightly gravelled path guided the way around the enclave.

"Create havoc, that's what the master said! Havoc!" Agga queried. "Yeh! You know mayhem! "Right mayhem!"

"Is the door open," Agga asked dumbly.

"Use your powers we don't need doors! "You just don't get it do you! Use your astral body to penetrate solid objects! Walk through walls!" Melchin declared vigorously.

The beautiful doves were nervous. Some were asleep, resting, hunched against each other, or in corners on perches, bobbing their heads up and down cooing and flapping their wings in alarming surprise. Some moving about sporadically like startled commuters at rush hour looking for a way out.

As the serene setting descended into chaos, the two apparitions projected themselves through the walls of the huge loft.

"That was easy!" cried Agga.

"Its wood, that's why. It's easier to penetrate you fool!" preached Melchin.

"OK, know all! Keep cool!. "Ooh lovely doves!" Agga sighed

"Kill them" Kill them all!" screeched Melchin. "You know the best way to kill a pigeon?"

"No what's that? asked Agga.

"Wring their necks? Wring their necks? Agga quizzed again.

"Yeh! Just grab one!"

The birds were now flying and fluttering over the heads of the ghouls, and all around in frustration and confusion. This was not what they were used to, they sensed a bad atmosphere, a terror not known to them! Not the loving kind and gentle aura of Luke, with his soothing hands and fresh food and water. This was something new.

"Grab one", Melchin ordered again. "Look, take your forefinger and middle finger and wrap it around the birds head. Then pull and twist hard." The bird fell dead, hanging limply down from the palms of Melchin's hands, its neck broken, limp and lifeless.

"Let's do them all! It'll be fun!"

Ten minutes later, every bird in the loft was dead. Feathers were strewn and scattered amongst the carcasses, blood seeping from some of the beaks of the 20 magnificent white doves. A true scene of carnage.

"All dead! All dead! Hee hee!" sniggered Melchin. "The boys next, let's go."

Glen and Rosa worked hard and today was no different. They had retired to their room, going through the usual routine of bedtime protocol. Shower, wash and comb, moisturise, a little exercise, check the fingernails, teeth, and glass of water on the side table, maybe a book. They were settled. No love-making tonight, but a gentle kiss and an embrace when they came close enough to be intimate in the confines of the spacious bedroom. The room was bathed in a pleasant glow, a soft light almost neon in radiance. Rosa, her hair tied back in a loose pony tail was naked under her silk deep blue negligee that rested itself upon her perfectly formed breasts.

Rosa and Glen froze as six visitants crowded through the walls like an army of wolves about to attack their prey. Their appearance was that of a living nightmare. Surrounded and devastated at the sight of something so atrocious, they almost lost their senses. The bath water was running, Mozart was playing softly on Glen's compact hi-fi. A hard day on the golf course had tempted Glen into a relaxing soak in the fragrant bath water. A lavender essence permeated the steamy air. There was no quarter given by the evil invaders.

The strength was in their phenomenal hidden magic. The influence of witchcraft and sorcery was a spell over the human race. Glen was semi-naked in his silky white monogrammed boxer shorts. Like winged serpents they grasped Glen by the arms and held him fast and strong. Two of the assailants restrained Rosa. Their lecherous gaze told of the sexual intent and molestation that was to be inflicted on their victim.

"She's a beauty", one said with an evil cackle. Guided by the droned devilish voice of Satan himself, the devotees carried out the instructions and lay Rosa on the mattress as the monstrous effigy appeared out of the ether. A vision of the macabre, a personification of hell's fury.

It spoke, "Make ready to receive your Lord and be grateful of the honour. Glen was a strong man but he was held fast by the four ghouls hovering in space five foot above the heart shaped bed, his legs dangling, kicking slightly against the supernatural power that the fiends had over him. His restrained body was almost motionless. The power of speech had left him.

It was an uncanny feeling, unnatural, unearthly, mystical like a trance. Only his eyes could focus on the rape and violation of his true love. The scene was set. Two more phantoms stood either side of the savage beast. Rosa's silky blue negligee lay open, the loose tags had been undone and the gown had been parted to reveal the most glorious sight, her naked body splayed for all to see. A curvaceous goddess of love. The oyster skin radiant and vibrant. Her breasts so full and rounded. Her areola complemented their perfect form, so dark and sultry against the flesh. Her finely toned torso ran like marble down to hips and a pelvis of sheer delight. The shapely trimmed mons verneris sat upon the most inviting labia majora. A vulva to die for. Her mount of Venus. So complete and erotic. Not unlike the petals of a sumptuous summer rose. It was time the devil himself was ready, standing looking down on his captive, the enslaved Rosa. He legs open, ready for his entrance into the sugared walls. She could see, she could feel, but could not speak or resist the atrocity which was to befall her sacred body. The beast readied itself. Its penis, bull-like and erect, was a foot long and two inches wide and throbbing. There she was stretched out at his mercy on the marital bed where she had loved so sweetly before.

The wind was howling, the misty rain and fog had cleared to reveal a silvery moon, but the clouds were dark and gloomy. When Tony arrived home and found that everyone had retired to their beds. He was enjoying a night cap from the drinks cabinet and had decamped to his room. It was a large Disarrono with fresh orange and a chunk of ice. His favourite cocktail. He was browsing, relaxed, glad to be home for the half term break, fingering the spines of the books on the ornate delicately carved mahogany bookcase, he'd had fitted. He had done some light training and showered and was now sitting on his bed in his smart, snug-fitting velcro gym shoes and loose fitting white satin Ju-Jitsu style lounge suit, with the rising sun (the emblem of Japan) emblazoned on the back. He had just finished the remnants of his drink when a scream shattered the tranquillity. His mother cried his name in fervent passion. The glass he held dropped to the deep thread carpet with a dull thud. Startled but ever alert and concerned he raced from his room, flinging the door open in a split second, leaping across the hall to his parents room. His face now spotted with perspiration. Fear and anxiety swamped his silhouette as the light flickered on and off in tormenting fashion. Though controlled as he always was, his panic was at its maximum. He reached the main bedroom, his heart pounding, beating like a drum against his chest. he pushed the door ajar. The dim light of intermittent neon barely broke the darkness. In flashes of lights he could make out his mother prostrate on the bed. Tony could make out two hooded figures either side of the divan.

"Stop" Tony yelled, like a sergeant major on the parade ground. The intruders, turning with a menacing look, arms enfolded across their breast bones, like they were at a sacrificial rite. They could cast their eyes on any object and it would fly with amazing speed. they could seek out the missiles, may it be a lamp, book, hairbrush or wall clocks, draws could fly out of cabinets, crashing into its target with ferocious power, splaying clothes and bric-a-brac in all direction. Tony could use his eye co-ordination and Ju-Jitsu moves to combat the onslaught, smashing the objects one by one with his amazing physical prowess blocking and parrying with feet, arms and hands. His speed and agility was astonishing. Not a cut or bruise was made upon his person. By this time the beast had retreated almost unnoticed into the shadows with the stealth and sorcery of transportation, he could appear and disappear at will in a millisecond. It was frightening. Six assailants approached. They were now fully formed. They had materialised and were now leaden foot on the solid surface of the grand bedroom.

Glen had been flung against an adjacent wall by the evil four that held him earlier. He lay semi conscious, groggy and concussed in pain. The predators were now more concerned with Tony.

Rosa was now returning to her natural state alert and lucid as she covered her modesty and raised herself from the bed disillusioned and distrtaught, she gathered her senses and responded to Glens cry for her to come close. Their hands met and they clung to each other with a trembling embrace. She brushed his hair with the palm of her hand, gazing into his eyes with concern and love.

Tony was now besieged by the group of foul, menacing, murderous assassins ready to tear him limb from limb. Ju-Jitsu is an amazing sport because that's what it is, a sport. The respect and conduct of this sport is unique. The honour and regard for peace and the karma of (ying and yang) is all-consuming, in the face of adversity. One is transcended to a level beyond this material world. In the aggressive physical action of battle, there is a calmness "Zen". the Japanese school of Mahavana Buddhism, emphasising the value of meditation and intuition. The art of Ju-Jitsu is to disarm and neutralise your opponent. The warrior in martial art takes the strength and power of his attacker and transfers it into his own, by form of light and dark, ying and yang, two complementary principles of philosophy. Ying is negative, dark and feminine. Yang is positive, bright and masculine. The components of martial arts (Ju-Jitsu) is to take the enemy's strength and use it for your own advantage. Some moves in the sport can throw a man or woman ten feet into the air such is the technique, balance and pressure, initiated in battle it can disorientate an opponent with spectacular results.

Two of the vile creatures made a move against Tony, grappling him by his arms. That was a mistake. In a split second Tony swirled his arms up and over like the sails of a windmill, thus reversing the actual motion of the foolish wraiths. With one move, he grasped their robes at the collar and smashed their heads full on into each other's. The devastation that occurred was tumultuous. Their skulls crashed together like egg shells, splintering into a multitude of fragmented pieces of opaque gruesome matter.

The sequence of moves and battle mode learnt in the process of martial arts is all-consuming. Techniques, structured patterns, assembled choreography is taught and practiced. A student learns to fight more than one opponent at a time. In fact, it can be as many as four, even six if need be. Back kicks, sweeping moves, arm locks, blocks, parrys, shoulder throws, roundhouse, kicks to torsos, heads, wrist locks. Counter measured against garrotting, breaking strangle chokes. Front kick, side kick, front snap kick. Two methods of escape when held over and under the arms back and front. Tremendous agility to combat all attackers.

Four more aggressors came forth, like they meant business. First, lightning bolts from their eyes sent Tony sprawling across the room, slamming into the recess of the bay window. He was immune to pain at this present time. Keeping low, he sprang from his low level position like a black panther aiming at the legs of the assailants, sweeping two of them off their feet with a glorious swirling move with his powerful right leg snapping one of the fiends legs in half. The other felled and stunned by the swift action of Tony. Two more hooded brutes swooped in on Tony as he clambered to his feet. Claws visible, one aimed for a strangle hold, and wrapped its cold withered hands around his neck in a death-like grip. In a flash of movement, Tony brought his forearm down over the top of the assailant's arms, breaking the hold completely to the astonishment of the creature, who was stunned into inertia.

Then, Tony, in the same move brought his forearm and fist back up into the haggard face of the ghostly apparition, obliterating totally the features of the horrendous bag of bones. The next unlucky vagabond to receive retribution was the last one standing. Stunned into silence and in shock, it stood motionless. Tony moved like lightening with a front snap kick to its groin. It was bent in torture not uttering a sound. Collapsing in a heap it was stone dead. There was still one more groaning on the floor from the previous encounter (the sweeping leg move). It was disillusioned and groggy. Tony picked the thing up, saw the bath of water lapping over the rim of the Jacuzzi-shaped tub. He carried it into the en-suite section, and sinking the devilish lump of garbage into the watery depths, drowned its sorry arse until the bubbles popped the surface for one last time.

Tony reappeared from the bathroom, one arm resting against the framed entrance. His Ju-Jitsu style garments soaked and slightly crumpled from the all out action. The bodies of the ghouls lay all about. Rosa and Glen were safe.

"Go," Tony said. "Get out of the house. It may not be safe."

There was not time for sentiment. His only concern was for the safeguard of his family.

"Go," he said again. "Ring the police".

Glen and Rosa made their way across the room, nodding in agreement at Tony and skipped down the stairs, holding one another tentatively as they went.

Tony surveyed the devastation. He relieved himself of his sodden, water drenched top, letting his hang by his side, contemplating the scene of destruction. His torso exuded the physique of an athlete. The toned muscles profoundly glistening with moisture. A 48 inch chest rose and sank with the even relaxed but, hyper-ventilative breathing. he though it was over.

A grunt and an exhale of breath, and a sickly stench emanated through the icy air. In a dark corner hidden in an eerie, shadowy light came the most horrific sight anyone could imagine. A heavy cloved foot thudded onto the bedroom floor, then another. Like a giant troll, demonic and devilish. But this, this horrible monster was not so benevolent. Not so humanoid. This thing was murderous and had the strength of ten men. This was Beezlebub himself, Satan Lord of misrule. The great barrel chest, the powerful arms and sinewy muscles, triceps and biceps bulging in a black shiny mass, from shoulders with massive deltoids baring down to claws. With nails of rigid steel protruding scimitar-like from the fingertips of gnarled hands. Legs with enormous thighs and calf muscles ended with the cloven feet, not unlike metamorphic rock. Its face bewitching with a huge hooked nose. Its eyes deep and hooded glowed with a red illuminous tint, piercing and hypnotic. The forehead was large, wide and deep, like a rocky mountain ridge, and topped with black wiry hair as of crimps. Short, stumpy ribbed horns ending in a dull point, bent outward to the ears, veiny and protruding. It's facial skin was the colour of an Amazon swamp. A pointed chin, chiselled with a profound cleft rose up in a slow determined manner. The thing looked down at Tony, with eyes cast and spoke in a deep baritone sound (not at all musical) echoing gravely from its black dark pit of a mouth. The teeth razor sharp and rancid. A gooey, greenish bile clung on for dear life, as the monstrosity sucked and slathered. The lips quivering with lascivious lust for bloody death and mayhem.

"You're quite a formidable foe, for a human", it spluttered. "Aren't you. All my friends have been destroyed, annihilated. Well! they're not my friends really, they're just useful. There's thousands where they came from. Ready to do my bidding. But it looks like I'll have to deal with you myself."

The voice had a slight timbre, a resonance. A little voice coaching would not go amiss Tony thought.

"You don't scare me, you bag of puss!" Tony exclaimed. He'd had enough nothing could deter him now. No creature, no spawn of hell, no freak of nature, no evil satanic mutant, half-brained and clumsy, misshapen clodhopper would get in his way now. Tony's adrenalin was now at its maximum. He was almost superhuman. Every fibre of his rigid body was in full battle mode. His moves, his thinking was lightening fast, breathtaking, astonishing fists of fury, flashing feet (with wings) could break a man's legs, ribs, arms. His moves, his skill were a lethal combination. Years of practice had turned him into a machine. A fighting machine of awesome power and precision.

Before the thing could move its putrid body, Tony half turned, then swivelled back on the ball of his left foot, sending out a lethal limb to the side of its head and temple. The instep of his right foot smashed side-on against the head of his opponent, crushing the cheekbone in the process. The kick was so powerful that it spun the hideous thing sideways, spinning. A sweeping move he had perfected in training. The monstrosity landed in a clump in the corner, crashing full on with the wall and angle of the room. Like a trapped bear it rose.

"That hurt!" it pronounced in a monotone garble. Tony had learnt one thing. Hesitate and the moment was lost. He'd read his mind and no harm would befall this warrior. He would be first to relinquish the enemy. It lumbered forward laboriously arms outstretched. Spittle dangling from the gaping orifice like a rabid dog ready to strike. Another blow, this time a frontal kick, with the accuracy of a missile to its contact. A short, sharp projected strike to the solar plexus with the full measure of his right foot brought the brute to bear the complete and utter power of the blow bent the ragged lump to its knees. Gasping for air in great clumps of breath. Tony stood over it like an executioner, looking on in disgust. The fiend was immobilised and there was only one way to finish this thing. He had to kill the beast. He grasped its arm, dragging it helpless and groaning out of the room and into his own sleeping quarters. There, hung a gleaming, shining Samurai sword in its ornate metal sheath, embossed with a dragon, and a emblem of the rising sun on its hilt. Still gasping for its breath, crumpled and forlorn, the body lay motionless. Taking the sword from off the wall over his bed, Tony unsheathed the blade. He held the sacred symbol and thought of the teachings and conduct revered by the masters of Ju-jitsu. Peace, honour, humility, respect and justice for the faint of heart. Peace in all manner of life serenity was the aim of the teachings. But this was different. This was peace shattered, torn and demonised. This had to be reckoned with, snuffed out, cleansed, purified. The zenith of his faith was in his hands. 'Zen' the teachings; the contemplation of one's essential nature to the exclusion of all else. The only way of achieving pure enlightenment. He raised the sword craftsman-like above his head. The beast must die!

Luke was still reading. It struck 12am on the ancient long-case clock in the main hall. A very gentle sound that actually calmed the soul. It resounded very harmoniously through the house. Luke could just hear the chimes when he thought it was time to put the books away and get some sleep. That would be enough of chemical analysis for tonight. He reached for the table lamp, as he looked up, feeling uneasy. He sat motionless, staring at a sight he imagined was due to his tiredness and mental stress. The visitants appeared through the walls about three feet above the floor then landed gently on their toes resting menacingly. They both had a white dove in the palms of their hands.

"Hello boy", said Melchin. "You're going to die, like these birdies of yours!"

The doves landed on the floor with a thud. Luke looked at the birds and tears filled his astonished eyes. He couldn't speak. The unspeakable had happened. Something that almost froze his heart to a stop, but then again to start it beating with utmost fear and revulsion at the horrifying spectacle revealed before him.

Alone and terrified, lost in the turmoil of the passing moments. Melchin pulled a knife from his belt—a dagger he used in his smuggling days. It was super sharp with a bone handle. It glinted in the light like a sabre in the sun.

Melchin spoke again, curling his lip. "This is for you young Luke! Hari Kari. Ever heard of Hari Kari Luke? All this school work. Surely you'd be better off dead! Take the knife boy!" he ordered.

The gruesome thing landed on Luke's bedcovers. It had a slight curve and a pointed tip.

"It would be easy wouldn't it boy? Just stick it in your belly and bleed to death, or slit your wrists that's fairly painless, BUT that would never do now would it. We need you to feel pain." Melchin's eyes widened as he prattled on.

Luke had had some low times in his life but never ever thought of committing suicide. His mother would never have forgiven him for that, and Dad would never have understood. As for Tony, well, it would be unthinkable.

Luke was dumbstruck. But a scream was building from the depths of his soul. His adrenalin was at its maximum.

"Well, do it, child, or I'll do it for you," Melchin growled and moved closer to the bed. Agga followed in a grovelling fashion.

"I've already killed two men!" Melching said proudly. "Clubbed them to death I did when we caused a ship to be wrecked on the rocks no so far from 'ere, in our smugglin' days. I' devils hole was out place on Hilbre Island wi' a cave 'n' all for the contraband and the loot. And now we are paying for our sins. 'Eh, Agga, aye this was the spot we let many a seafarer die, drowned and maimed but we had the booty 'eh, Agga."

"Yeh, Melchin," Agga replied, "And a sorry time it was. I think my soul is damned forever! Cursed as I am in this state. Ragged and disease-ridden! and we don't even get our proper names! Agga! What's that? My name is George!"

"Aye, 'n' my name is Henry," chirped in Melchin. "They won't give us our real names where we come from young 'un. We don't deserve it. We have to suffer you see. But now you have to suffer! Come on boy, use the dagger. Slit your wrists, blood! Let's see some blood."

"Tony!!!" Luke screamed at the top of his voice.

Luke had suspected that Tony was home. He'd heard the faint close of the huge oak door through his open window. Visitors would be greeted by sleek white marble steps bevelled outwards in a fan shape to an open spaced hall. The sprawling staircase welcomed one like a friend with open arms. The winding tread ever growing wider with banisters splaying out left and right, one towards the lounge, the other toward the drawing room. The balustrades ending in a swirling knot like pools of ebony coloured water, grand and majestic. An enormous Persian carpet swamped the entrance of the hallway. Antique hat and coat stands graced either side of the threshold. Sweet ferns sprang upwards from large decorative jardinières, nestling alongside umbrella racks. A crystal chandelier hung dead centre over a balsa wood disc-shaped tabled. Pure red roses in a floral pattern sat snugly in a china vase atop a pure white cotton doily. The long case clock was in a recess near to the drawing room.

The room Luke slept in was (as I've mentioned) small in comparison to the rest of the house. If there was to have been a nursery, then this was it. But considering that no more children were on the horizon, Luke was happy to stay put. He was a creature of habit and had everything he needed. Twenty two inch flat screen TV, Game Boy, writing desk, computer console, dressing table, vanity unit, built in wardrobes with a full length mirror, exercise bike, a single bed with a teak bedside cabinet and reading lamp. The famous photo of Albert Einstein (slightly perplexed in his study) was framed above the headboard. Double doors opened up onto a spacious areas with an oblong coffee table and lounge chair, a little like the oval office in the "White House" with wood panelled wall and a dormer window (but on a much smaller scale).

Tony hesitated. Luke's cry penetrated his senses and rang in his ears. Alarmed, but subdued he looked down to the trophy he though he held, stunned and amazed. He was now staring at a vacant, empty space. The monstrosity had vanished in the blink of an eye. Tony's only thought now was for Luke. He race through the door and on down the hallway. Sword still in hand, he burst into Luke's room blazing with contempt. The intrusion of these fiends would not be tolerated for one moment. Luke called out to Tony in a saddened cry.

Looking at him for guidance and direction, "Tony, Tony," he implored. The ghostly apparitions turned in unison.

"Hello, and who are you?" they said in a chorus, giggling, looking at each other, then at Tony again.

"I'll show you who I am!" Tony called back, smirking almost comically. In a single movement he brought the gleaming, sparkling and flashing Samurai sweeping, swishing through the air like an arrow. It pierced the hideous creature clean through the heart. It stood for a second or two, erect and then crumpled to its knees, sinking to its haunches. It sat there like a waxworks dummy staring into oblivion. One more unexpected guest to deal with and this was done in spectacular fashion.

Before the alien could muster a thought Tony projected himself into the air with a flying, masterful scissor-kick which succeeded in almost tearing the head off the shoulders of the bewildered tramp-like figure. It dropped to the floor like a ragdoll.

Two more apparitions materialised through the walls, floating in mid air, looming over Tony like banshees. A lightening strike flashed from their fingertips sending Tony rocking back on his heels. They came closer, grabbing Tony by the arms, ready to throw him through the window which was blown open. The moon shone like a beacon.

They moved forward ready to eject Tony from the sill to the spiked railings below. But in one magnificent move he cart-wheeled his legs over his shoulders therefore twisting his arms out of the grip of the fiends, who had pure hatred in their faces. He landed perfectly on his feet and made his stance. The ghouls were so shocked by his movement, they floated in mid air and just gazed at each other in bewilderment. This was Tony's moment. In one movement he projected himself up in a leap with his right leg rigid like a ninja in full fight. This connected so amazingly well with the torso of one of the demons that it sent the thing flying through the window itself. His next move as he landed firmly on his feet was to swivel on his left foot, swooping his right limb around in a 45 degree angle sending it crashing into the face and head of the second opponent and this sent the gruesome spectre careering against the adjacent wall. A powdery dust flew in all directions. Tony stood in fighting mode, Ju Jitsu-style, waiting for its next move. Crumpled and with its head partly ripped from its shoulders it was in no condition to fight back.

Moving toward the window, tony looked over the sill and a sight froze him to the core. There, impaled on the spiked railing below, was the other demon hanging with a spike directly through its heart, splayed like a fish on a spear, arms and legs dangling, a red glutinous resin dripping slowly down its arms and onto the pavement below.

The thing with ghosts and phantoms, they're from another world, another realm, another sphere of reality. They live in their own special atmosphere, they can move in a formidable way as in a way that UFO's are said to be able to using their power over matter. The force of gravity does not apply. But their magic powers tend to dissipate with time the longer they stay on earth. They morph into a solid being, losing their ethereal lightness and powers. Their bodies become as one, any limbs not apparent may appear gradually as their form begins to relate to the world's biospheric fusion.

The biophysics of the troposphere. The morphology. Morphogenesis, in fact metamorphosis within the elements of their molecular structure. This applies to zombies, phantoms, spectres, poltergeists. Some visitants can leave evidence of their visit like pools of water or a gooey horrible mess of slime, ectoplasm, or spontaneous combustion (a pile of ashes).

Two more phantom like zombies transported themselves through the walls of the annex (Rosa' study). An accumulation of shiny ribbons, buttons and bows, belts, togs and tassels. Silk and satin gossamer chiffon, crimplene, rolls of velvet, nylon, polyester, serge, cheesecloth, denim, muslin, roll upon roll of fabric on shelves of shiny mahogany, like colours of the rainbow blending into a fabulous mosaic.

Cotton reels, sewing machines (2), boxes of clasps, rings, buckles, lacey collars and cuffs. Jewellery, glitter in assorted shades, blue, red, green haute couture at the highest level. The misbegotten ragged wraiths began their carnage. "Pretty frilly! Pretty frilly!" one pronounced in a sickly high despicable scolding voice, like the wicked witch in her wooded coven. "Hubble bubble toil and trouble" it exclaimed again giggling and cackling, tossing the glimmering, glistening, brightly coloured ribbons up in the air with it's dirty pot marked emaciated hands, the long fingernails congealed with dirt and blood. "Burn the place down, burn, burn, burn!". His similarly pathetic companion stood in silence watching the spectacle unfold. "Fire" the first one said again "Fire!". The tall gangly accomplice stepped back and with the most horrid piercing dark red and glowing eyes, let out a bolt of light like a laser beam. The power unleashed egnighted the flimsy delicate structure of the material. The flames took hold, rampant like a bush fire. "Lets get out of here!" they both said so comically. They vanished through walls once again disappearing into the remnants of mist that still lingered in the thickness of trees surrounding the mansion, their ghost like figures fading away to nothing amid the denseness of smog. The fire was so fierce that the whole room of the annex was a flame. But the water sprinklers were in operation and the smoke detectors sounded their shrill deafening, earth shattering alarm. Mayhem still reigned at the Barrington household.

Glen's trembling hand reached for the phone on the white marbled topped ornate table in the hall and punched in the numbers 999. Rosa drew closer and hugged him round the waist nuzzling into his chest and shoulder. He raised his free arm and held her tight "My God!" cried Rosa "There's a fire, oh no not my workshop Glen!". She glanced up at her husband "Not the workshop!" she said again. She grasped him fiercely "Not the workshop!" Clinging to his semi naked body, the tears welled up in Rosa's eyes and stained his bare chest. She wept uncontrollably.

Smoke was gathering in the hall, billowing, oozing its deadly toxins along the floor and up the walls. The smoke alarms still blaring their distressing racket. Glen was seething, his lips were sealed tight and his teeth were clenched with rage. His hand still trembled but he held the phone fast with a strong grip.

A female operator answered the call.

"Hello, Merseyside Police, how can I help you?"

Glen stayed calm. His army training came into play "Please come quickly, we're being attacked by the forces of evil, we need the police, the fire brigade and the paramedics".

"Ok, sir, please stay calm and give me your name, address and location, spelling out any unusual names or words". Glen spoke clearly and precise giving her the information she required. The operative spoke again "Is there anyone hurt or in need of immediate assistance?". "I'm not certain" replied Glen. "We're a little shaken up. I'm not sure if we're safe. Please hurry, the house is on fire".

"We'll be there as soon as possible" the operator assured him.

Glen put down the phone and looked up. There at the top of the stairs were his sons.

Tony had appeared at the top of the stairway, his hand on Luke's shoulder, holding him firmly and safely at arms length looking down the staircase at his distraught parents. The sight of Luke and Tony safe and sound was a consolation amid the turmoil. Tony looked like a greek god. His naked torso gleaming in the glow of the chandelier, statuesque like polished marble. His stomach muscles ribbed like hewned granite. "Go Luke, go into the courtyard, take mum and dad!". "But you have to come too" cried Luke in desperation at leaving his beloved brother alone. "No Luke, go now, I'll be safe, I have to check everything is ok and under control, don't worry my mate, I'll be there soon. Please go quickly and wait for the Police". "I will open the gates", Luke leapt the tread of the stairs, two at a time. "Mum, Dad, let's go!". Luke grasped his mother's hand. "Come mum, we'll be safe outside, Dad hurry!" Luke wailed but with a renewed confidence in his voice.

Tony followed the smoke down the hall to Rosa's study. Her pride and joy, her refuge, her life's work. He checked the smoke and fire damage. The fire had ceased, the sprinklers had done their job. The shocking destruction that had occurred was now diminished, only smouldering embers flickering in corners on shelves, ashes and black sludge covered almost every part of the annexe. Everything was tarnished. Most things completely ruined and worthless. The water was ankle deep, dripping off tables down curtains, walls, sodden rolls of material damaged beyond rescue. Mannequins black and half burned lay around like dead bodies in a war zone.

Tony reached for the fire extinguisher outside in a recess on the wall and quenched the last of the flames that flickered here and there. Mum could not be witness to the carnage and wreckage that would be so heart rendering. Tony closed the door with a saddened sigh, blood still coursing through his rampant veins.

Michael Wilson supervised the situation himself, the impression that was given and relayed to the waiting officers was that a substantial family (The Barringtons of Seacombe) were being attacked by a person or persons unknown. The Barringtons were known to the Police and the Police Chief on duty that night (Michael Wilson) knew Glen Barrington personally, from the local golf club and through dealings within the Borough.

"This sounds a bit weird lads but we need to check this out!" he preached to his staff. "Take an armed response team, we're not taking any chances on this one".

A Sergeant with his three stripes glinting on his epaulettes, showed the way. Neil Turner was a man not to be reckoned with. He would see the job through. He spoke to his fellow constables as he sped to the panda cars, readied and waiting in the stations car park.

"It could be a break in. It could be revelers, we don't know. Considering the date this may seem like a practical joke but we believe the source to be genuine. It's not a scam boys. This is a priority number, it's well known to the establishment. Treat it with respect, let's go!".

Police sirens were wailing through the street and roads of the peaceful town. Ambulances spend in hot pursuit, their blue spinning warning lights flashing furiously. Roaring through the gates at Rosslyn Manor they almost skidded to a halt, their tyres grating crushing against the gravely track surrounding the giant water feature.

A helicopter whirled its blades noisily above. Its massive searchlight beamed down its almighty blinding glow creating an eerie presence in the fog, and woods of the Manor. Circling the perimeter as it swooped and swayed its way across and around the property. The whole area was alive with S.O.C.O. (Scene of Crime Officers) Police tapes (cordons), flashing lights, police cars, ambulances (2) policemen, paramedics, firemen, fire engines (3), one at the gate, two parked in the grounds either side of the fountain. Two panda cars were parked at the main entrance to the house the whole façade was lit by the security lighting that was recently installed. It flooded the courtyard like it was day. Hoses resembling giant pythons wriggling and writhing, lined their way toward the gaping portal and into the confined of the smouldering smoke filled regency styled residence. (Chaos reigned). Men carrying stretchers dressed in light blue transparent jump suits, and white surgical gloves, (plastic overshoes protecting their footwear) ran in and out of the mansion. Body bags were being hauled into a black maria. Police chiefs and lesser denominations chatted and conversed feet away in the shadows. Two constables stood at the entrance both sides of the threshold. Their hands clasped behind their back peering straight ahead. Tony stood staring into the void. Hands by his sides fists clenched tight in fury. Still topless and naked from the waist up. He was being attended to by a paramedic, who was shining a small laser type flashlight into his eyes, (checking for vital signs). Tony blinked at the intrusion turning his head at an angle. A policeman tried covering his shoulders with a blanket. Tony flinched slightly waving him away. The Officer looked quizingly, but with concern and admiration, and nodded affirmatively going about his duties!

A young attractive police woman had her arm around Luke's shoulders in the back of an ambulance which was stationed a little way down the white gravel path leading to the house and fountain. A silver coloured thermal sheet covered his body. He'd had the courage and the fortitude to rescue two newly born off springs from the Dovecote. His eyes were full and glossed over with a fine moisture, slight tear stains marked his cheeks. The carnage inside the Dovecote was too much for his sensitive caring nature.

First into the house was the senior fire officer to check the damage. Closely followed by the armed response team guns drawn. "Everything is secured the fire is out, there is no more perpetrators in the vicinity only dead ones!" said the sergeant with raised eyebrows and a look of astonishment. "My men are searching the grounds as we speak". The sergeant shook Glen's hand. "Are you feeling well enough to tell me a little more about what's happened? Some more information would be useful. We've never come across this sort of thing before, you know the supernatural and the likes!". The sergeant gestured frowning "It's a bit strange to say the least. I think its best if we keep this quiet, don't want to alarm the neighbourhood, the tabloids would have a field day!".

It was over, the terrifying ordeal. The disturbing sequence of events that infiltrated the tranquil, unhindered world of the Barrington family. The mortifying aspects of supernatural occurrences, that invade, that destroy, that impair, that spoil and hinder the natural course of human endeavour. The evil that resides within mankind and the human element. The infidelities that persist, that harm the malevolent structure that exists in the Universe. Unleashed in waves of torment and terror in all manner of existence. Solitary trust, honour and faith. The badges of courage. Fortitude hope, the balance that must tip the scales in favour of happiness, caring and constructive living. That great mountain that must be climbed in order to reach a summit of contentment. The honesty and beauty of true glorious enlightenment. "Love!".

There was an unimaginable peacefulness, a tranquillity, a stillness. Tony could actually hear his heart beating like it was echoing through the night air and into the vastness of space and time. In that one moment in a split second there came a roar, an incarnation. The horrendous figure of Beelzebub came screaming out of the darkness. Breathing belching smoke and spewing flames from the black pit of its gaping hole of a mouth. Flying in a loathsome, despairing attack, with Tony in its sights, like a raging wounded bear, growling, screeching hatred and vicious death. "Die human die!". Tony was almost god like as he focused on this image of hell. The thing reached him, claws visible, arms outstretched. Tony in one complete incredible motion blocked one arm and taking hold of it's body swooped his other arm around its torso and in one momentous move demonstrated the complete power and force of a full hip throw. The speed and momentum that the devil had implemented created energy and drive so that Tony's astonishing technique propelled the hideous monstrosity twenty feet trough the air. The lump of vile flesh, the ugly putrid mass flew through the spacious confines of the court yard. Flailing its arms and legs. It was almost like slow motion as Tony watched it's body careering towards the fountain and the statue of Eros. Landing full force on top of the ancient symbol of love. The God of Love, son of Aphrodite. A scream, and an emanation of blue and red phosphorous light receded into the atmosphere and dark empty sky. Leaving its body impaled on the statue like a side of beef with arms and legs dangling down toward the rippling water of the fountain. "NOW IT WAS OVER!"

The congregation were stunned. The action that took place was over in seconds. It stopped all proceedings. Guns were drawn by the task force. They stood with their pistols pointing forward both hands holding their weapons strong and firm, crouched legs akimbo, eyes fixed on the target ahead that had not moved a muscle. They surrounded the grotesque figure in the fountain steadily approaching it tentatively inch by inch. One officer climbed into the moat and prodded the fiendish brute with the nuzzle of his hand gun to see if there was any signs of life. A snort, an exhale of breath and more blood like black bile oozed from its grisly steaming carcase.

In an instant the officer now up to his knees in water fired six bullets into it's brain from close range. The sound of bullets being fired eminated through the icy moist air, resembling the crack of a whip. Inspector Wilson pulled Sergeant Turner to one side and spoke. "We need a priest and a psychologist get the family into a top hotel in the area, these people have been through enough, contact any relatives. I will talk to Glen Barrington myself and find out the name of his insurance company. Carry on Sergeant!" Neil Turner went about his duties.

Luke held the two baby chicks in the palms of his trembling hands, cold and disillusioned, terror struck and forlorn, but he was safe in a police car. These two baby doves would be his Phoenix, rising from the ashes. His ray of hope, his quest for peace and solidarity. His hope for the future. His magic formula for a happy and contented existence. Love, honour and peace in a world filled with harmony, justice and faith.

Glen looked into Rosa's clear pearl-grey sparkling eyes. They were in each other's arms there in the courtyard.

"We'll rebuild, bigger, better," he pronounced proudly, looking up, glancing at the partly smouldering devastation. She hugged him tight.

"As long as I have you by my side and the love of my family I'm the happiest woman in the world". He cupped her face within his strong gentle hands.

"I love you so much", he said. His eyes filled with tears as he kissed her lips so gently and tenderly.

And there it was "Rosslyn" emblazoned over the portal until eternity decides its fate or the brickwork crumbles into dust.

Tony looked up to the skies unintentionally and a vision materialised. Two glorious, giant angels swooped down and over the rooftops glowing with iridescent white light. Their angelic faces like alabaster shone with a beauty no man could put into words. A manifestation of heaven, a personification of Gods immaculate, productive power, purity immortalised, instilled in heavenly bodies that was beyond comprehension.

Angels of the night, translucent in gossamer enchanting beyond compare. A welcome spectre, and the promise of Elysian Fields to come.

EPILOGUE

There was a finality in the time that elapsed, a winding down, a closure. The birds began their dawn twitter, the chorus began one or two at a time in the distant woods, a single note here and there. Then a full blown crescendo. Life was emerging back to its common customary state of play. Two officers remained at the main gates after replacing the night shift crew. A lone scientific support representative stayed on at the mansion for further investigation. The last of the salvage corps made their way out of the grounds leaving a garbage strewn lawn scattered with furniture, bric-a-brac and smouldering sodden reels of cloth, curtains desk tops lampshades, tables chairs, part burnt timbers. The windows of Rosa's study were blown out. The flames at one time were so fierce, they leapt the walls of the stately manor leaving dark stains streaking upwards towards the roof of the property. A ram-shackled ruination of pristine, historic seventeen century architecture. The wrath of life's demented sting had descended on an evil wind.

IS THIS STORY TRUE?

Lightning Source UK Ltd.
Milton Keynes UK
UKOW01f0437290916

284073UK00001B/86/P